ABOUT THE AUTHO

George G. Gilman was b
a small village east of Lo
schools until the age of fi
decided to become a professional writer, with strong
leanings towards the mystery novel. Wrote short stories
and books during evenings, lunch hours, at weekends,
and on the time of various employers while he worked
for an international newsagency, a film company, a
weekly book-trade magazine and the Royal Air Force.

His first short (love) story was published when he was
sixteen and the first (mystery) novel appeared ten years
later. He has been a full-time writer since 1970, writing
mostly Westerns which have been translated into a
dozen languages and have sold in excess of 16 million
copies. He is married and lives on the Dorset coast,
which is as far west as he intends to move right now.

The EDGE series by George G. Gilman,
published by New English Library.

A TIME FOR KILLING

George G. Gilman

NEW ENGLISH LIBRARY

A New English Library Original Publication, 1986

First NEL Paperback Edition February 1986

NEL Books are published by
New English Library
Mill Road, Dunton Green,
Sevenoaks, Kent.
Editorial office: 47 Bedford Square, London WC1B 3DP

Typeset by Rowland Phototypesetting Ltd
Bury St Edmunds, Suffolk

Printed in Great Britain by
Hunt Barnard Printing Ltd,
Aylesbury, Bucks

British Library C.I.P.

Gilman, George G.
   A time for killing. – (Edge; 51)
   Rn: Terry Harknett   I. Title   II. Series
   823'.914[F]   PR6057.I62

   ISBN 0-450-05901-4

for
C.C.
who discovered with relief
that I am not at all like
Edge.

One

EDGE AWOKE with an insistent pounding inside his skull, but even as he cracked open his eyes to catch a first glimpse of the bright light of a new day he knew that what ailed him was self-inflicted. This time nobody had cracked him over the head with a shovel or winged him with a long range rifle shot. He had simply drunk too much of Donald Kemp's corn-liquor-laced cider last night.

The brightness of the early morning sun intensified the sharpness of the pain between each dull thud of something that seemed to be trying to beat a way out from under his skull – a pain that was eased when he snapped his eyes closed. The leading arc of that same west Texas sun was almost touching the jagged ridge of one of the Eagle Mountains when he first saw the smoke of a small fire yesterday.

He was riding south east, not following any trail. Close to sixty miles and almost four days out of El Paso. A drifting saddletramp who was convinced deep down that he had taken more than his fill of people. Enough to last him a lifetime. And, he was just as positive, the more he stayed clear of his fellow human beings, the better was the chance of that lifetime being a long one.

It was not a fresh viewpoint from which to survey the world at large for the loner called Edge. Thus he was fully aware of the risk he ran when he veered his mount away from the direction he had been riding all afternoon to put

1

his back to the setting sun. Headed toward the column of grey woodsmoke that he knew was sent skywards from a fire not so far from the town of Pomona. Not in town, for many fires would have been kept burning in stoves and grates throughout the crisply cold late November day now drawing toward a colder evening. And the pall this would form in the chill and otherwise clear air was lost to sight beyond the humped rises of the Wylie Mountains foothills which now sprawled ahead of him.

Pomona was over in that direction someplace, he knew. With the entire state of Texas spread out beyond. While in back of him now, on the other side of the Eagle Mountains, was the Rio Grande that marked the border with Mexico. He knew such general facts about his surroundings because he had an intelligent grasp of the geography of his native land. Plus an innate sense of direction. Local knowledge of this piece of country he had never ridden before was picked up accidentally or deliberately while he drifted through it, constantly conscious of the way he was headed but infrequently having a specific destination in mind. Maybe a sheltered spot to bed down for the night; or a patch of good grazing where the chestnut gelding could feed as well as rest for a noonday break; or a column of smoke that signalled a fire where a man might be welcome to share the warmth on a winter's night and maybe have some hot food, too.

The sun that cast shadows at grotesque lengths in front of the rider and mount had shaded from pale yellow to deep crimson and was half hidden by the ridge when Edge saw the smoke rise from a fieldstone chimney on the outside end wall of a small farmhouse. This as he reached the rim of a broad, shallow hollow some half mile away from the place, and headed the gelding down the gentle incline without pause.

He was approaching the farmstead from the rear and he guessed it was unlikely many visitors stopped by from this direction. But the closer he rode the more his first

2

impression of the house, the out-buildings, the corral and the crop fields and orchards was reinforced. Everything was a long way from being brand, spanking new, but over the several years since roots had first been put down here there had been no let up in effort to tend the land, and the care for what had been erected upon it with farming skill had a high regard for good order.

The whole place, inside as well as out he guessed, would be immaculate. For the fact that there was no unsightly mess of junk and garbage heaped out back suggested nothing was done here simply to create a good impression. The people who lived here had a clean place for everything and everything was kept neatly in its place.

The house was of timber and stone construction, one story high with a low-pitched roof of tile. It had been added to over the years, and could now have as many as four rooms if none of them was extravagantly large. It faced north east and to the left of the front yard was an all-timber barn that was high enough to have a hayloft. Across from the barn was a second timber out-building that was maybe a stable. Out back of the stable and barn were fields that extended over some ten acres: most of them ploughed and fallow at this time of year but some seeded with crops of winter wheat or barley. A wagon-wide stretch of hard-packed dirt cut an arrow-straight path between the front yard and the trail that Edge knew linked the nearby town of Pomona with far distant El Paso. Just this stage trail marked the property boundary on this side. Elsewhere, lines of trees had been planted – the neatness of their alignment and the equal distances between them showing they had not been established there without the aid of the tidy-minded folks who lived and worked within the bounds they set.

These young poplars and elms and oaks and mixed firs were not the only types of tree down in the carefully husbanded bottom land of the hollow. For there were two orchards of fruit trees at the rear of the house, one to either side of a white-fenced corral. Because it was November, the trees were bare of leaves: likewise the corral was empty of stock. The corral was not large and probably was used for two or three horses and maybe a milk cow, Edge guessed as he rode between two tall firs and onto the property. A little later, as he drew close enough to the buildings for the distinctive fragrance of over-ripe apples to compete with the smell of woodsmoke, he knew what fruit was borne by the regimented rows of some fifty or sixty trees in each orchard.

Between the gated front fence of the corral and the rear wall of the house in which there were three windows and a door, a kitchen garden was as well kept as everything else on the farmstead. Rows of winter greenstuff and the tops of root crops grew in the finely tilled soil in perfectly straight lines without a weed seedling between them.

And as Edge reined in his mount after the final ray of sunlight disappeared from the hollow and the shadows of man and horse became lost in the evening, he felt strangely out of place: an unkempt, heavily travel-stained intruder who could surely not expect to receive a warm welcome to such a place as this. And maybe there was a much better than even chance that the people who lived here would not be overjoyed to greet him. But such circumstances he normally took for granted. This evening he found he was uncomfortably aware of being not a part of his surroundings. And this self-consciousness disturbed him to such a degree that he began to regret veering off his chosen course to ride toward the column of smoke. But then a narrow strip of lamplight showed at the base of the doorway and a moment later as the door was swung open, into the house, a man greeted in an amiable tone:

'Howdy, mister. You look in need of a place to rest up awhile. And if that's how it is, you're entirely welcome to rest up here.'

'Supper will be on the table before you know it, sir,' a

4

woman added and sounded even more eagerly welcoming than the man.

'But there'll be time enough for you to wash up, stranger,' a second, older woman put in quickly. Then hurried to qualify: 'If you've a mind to, that is?'

The man, holding the kerosene lamp, flanked by the women, crowded on to the threshold of the rear doorway and peered smilingly out at their evening visitor. And if any of them were disturbed by what they saw, close to, in the brightness of the yellow lamplight, it did not show.

What they saw was a man who, at the end of another long day's ride on a trail that stretched back over several such days, could have been aged from forty to fifty. Close to halfway was correct. A man with a sparsely-fleshed face that was sculptured and coloured by the merging of two racial bloodlines at his conception. His father had been Mexican and his mother had come from Scandinavia, although as often as not he was mistaken for a half-breed Indian: this because he elected to wear his once jet black hair, now streaked with grey, at a length that brushed his shoulders. It was a face darkened by heritage and exposure to the elements, with ice-blue eyes that glinted from between permanently narrowed lids, high cheekbones, an aquiline nose, wide and thin-lipped mouth and a slightly jutted jaw. His skin was deeply scored with the kind of lines that implied they were cut as much by the experiences of past years as by the number of those years. Because the day was drawing to a close, his lower face was thickly bristled: so that it was just possible to discern the line of a Mexican-style moustache.

He weighed in the region of two hundred pounds, leanly distributed over a frame of six feet two inches. He was dressed in the manner of the kind he looked to be, in mainly dark-hued clothing that was powdered by lighter-coloured trail dust from his plain-banded Stetson down to the spurless riding boots he wore inside his pants cuffs. Because it was cold weather, he had donned a sheepskin coat. But

5

he rode with it open, so the trio at the rear doorway of the farmhouse could see there was a bullet-heavy gunbelt encircling his waist. If they knew about firearms, they would recognise that the unfancy revolver in the holster tied down to his right thigh was a Frontier Colt.

The rifle that jutted from the boot slung on the front right side of his saddle was a Winchester. Elsewhere on the Western saddle were stowed the accoutrements necessary for a long ride over rough and sparsely-populated country. The saddle was on the back of a chestnut gelding that looked no more weary than it should have done after a day of easy riding by a man who understood the needs and the limitations of his mount.

If the stranger had an affectation in his appearance – outside of the underplayed moustache that drooped to either side of his mouthline – it was a necklet of dull-coloured beads that was partially visible between his jawline and the loosely knotted kerchief.

His face remained disconcertingly impassive for the few seconds it took for the man and two women to offer their friendly greetings and cautiously survey him from out of their smiling eyes. Then he expressed a smile of his own as he touched the underside of his hat brim with the knuckles of a half formed fist and replied:

'I'm obliged. For my horse, too. We're both in need of what you have to offer. But I need to pay for what we have.'

'Wouldn't hear of you doin' that, mister,' the man argued. Both he and the older of the women had slight accents. His was the stronger and Edge thought they originated from somewhere in northern Europe.

The fleeting smile drifted rather than swept off the half-breed's face as he answered in an even tone: 'Then I'm still obliged for the offer, but I'll be riding on.'

The man was in his mid-fifties. He was not tall and was stockily built with a bulge at his belly the only obvious sign of soft fat. He had a round, element-burnished face under thinning sandy hair. His eyes were of the same blue coloration as those of Edge, but suggested the farmer's warmth of personality instead of the ice-cold hardness that was truly seen in those of the half-breed. But there was, in the stance of the older man, in the way he held his head high and in the obvious physical strength he commanded despite the middle-aged spread, an undeniable warning that nobody should play him for a fool and expect to get away with it. Like the women, he was freshly washed-up from his chores of the day. He wore denim pants that had seen many better days and a checked shirt buttoned to the collarless neck that was much newer. His footwear was a pair of carpet slippers that looked close to new.

The older woman was close to his age, just a little younger. A half a head taller, she had a thin and angular build that was matched by her face. Perhaps in the old days she had toiled almost as long as the man in the fields and orchards of the place. But latterly, her complexion suggested, she spent most of the days out of the weather. Just as the man was not and probably never had been handsome, so the woman to his right had always been homely: because her greyish eyes were too small and too close together, her nose was sharply pointed and her lips lacked fullness. Maybe once the now-emaciated lines of her body had been sensually slender. Her eyebrows revealed that the now silver hair she wore in a bun was once black.

The younger woman, who was a little on the wrong side of thirty, had that kind of far less than full blown figure which Edge found attractive. But her face was no match for her body. It was round and a little puffy, the skin blemished by the scars of ancient acne. Her eyes were the same colour as those of the man, but were placed and shaped like those of the older woman. She had fine, very white teeth. Her hair was a mixture of auburn and blonde, lacked fullness and was cut severely short as if to stress its unbecoming straightness.

7

Both women were identically garbed in grey dresses that contoured without hugging their upper bodies and then swept loosely to their ankles from the tight waists. Waist aprons, again plain grey, also reached down to brush the polished tops of their unstylish footwear. Both had rolled up their sleeves to above the mid-forearm to protect the cuffs while supper was prepared.

'Admire a man who has his principles, stranger. And all three of us think the same way. Know it would be wrong to encourage you to go against what you believe in. Be happy for you to share in what we have. Just as happy to accept payment if that's your wish.' The older woman's smile had gone the same way as that of the half-breed and her tone of voice was in keeping with the indifferent expression that now sat easily on her thin face.

The man and the younger woman abruptly seemed anxious: for different reasons, Edge guessed. And this was confirmed after the older woman had backed in off the threshold and turned to hurry out of sight, murmuring softly about the need to attend to the stew.

'You could ride to Pomona in less than an hour without rushing,' the other woman suggested, with an unladylike gesture of a hooked thumb to indicate the direction of the nearest town. And there was in her unsmiling eyes a brand of plea that he should do just that: before she swung out of the doorway to go help with the interrupted preparations for supper.

'Hey now, don't you pay too much mind to what Annie says, mister,' the man urged. 'That's our daughter. Me, I'm Donald Kemp. What the wife said – she's Edwina, by the by – is how I think, too.'

He tried to make a fresh smile as warmly welcoming as the first one had been. But the expression that resulted was something akin to that which can be seen in the eyes of an anxious-to-please dog eager to be asked to perform a good deed for which it will get a reward.

'Name's Edge,' the half-breed supplied and swung

cautiously out of the saddle, flexing wearied muscles as he did so. 'You want to show me where I can bed down my horse for awhile and wash up and I'll –'

'Sure thing, Mr Edge,' Kemp agreed as he set down the lamp on something just inside the rear doorway and emerged from the house. Now he was as genuinely happy as before as he pulled the door closed behind him and beckoned for the half-breed to follow him. But he lowered his voice so that it was just audible above the clop of the gelding's hooves when he explained: 'I guess that girl must be gettin' close to her time of the month again, if you know what I mean? Changes her moods faster than a rattler can strike when her time's about due. Comes of her bein' still unmarried at her age, the wife says. But that's not her fault, I guess. Edge, you say? Friends call me Don. You got a name –'

'Not any more, feller. Just Edge is all.'

They had reached the front yard of the house, at the corner of the building the half-breed had presumed was a stable. But it was not the smell of animals that emerged from the cracks at the centre and top and base of the fastened double doors. For it was the cloying odour of over-ripe fruit, laced by a more subtle fragrance, that had its source within the building.

'I guess you're a man who takes a drink when the mood strikes him, Mr Edge?' Kemp suggested and there was a knowing grin on his round face now: after he had seen his visitor give the stable-like building a second glance of more than casual interest.

'The smell of rotten apples could kill my thirst for the corn liquor I figure I can smell in there, too?'

The stockily built farmer nodded and vented a short laugh as he beckoned for Edge to bring his horse between the corner of the house and a well. 'The corn liquor's a little strong for my taste. Need to tame it down with some cider.'

Lamplight from one of the four windows at the porched

9

front of the house angled a shaft over the yard until Annie
Kemp jerked a heavy drape across in back of the fine lace
curtain. But already the threequarters moon, low in the
sky, was bright enough to show Edge that the now leafless
summer-shade oak tree at the centre of the hard-packed
area was the only thing on the place – living or inanimate
– that did not conform to the Kemp family's obsession for
good order. It grew as nature intended, like this was its
privilege as the oldest inhabitant on the property. Whereas
the well was encircled by a neatly built, three-feet-high
stone wall upon which was a square timber arch support
for the winch that smelled of fresh grease. And the stable
that had become a distillery and the facing barn were set
at perfect right angles to the front of the house. Both
out-buildings had two windows each that faced the yard,
and the glass in them gleamed from as much polishing as
those of the house received. But, at least, they were not
hung with any kind of curtain.

'Make the liquor just for myself and our guests,' Kemp
went on as he opened one of a pair of doors near the front
end of the barn, beneath a block and tackle beam jutting
from the gabled entrance of the hayloft. The door swung
silently on recently oiled hinges and the garrulous farmer
strode confidently into the darkened interior: knew pre-
cisely where the lamp was stowed and was sure that nothing
would have been carelessly left in his path. 'Press the cider
for sale to Pomona folks. Or anybody else that has a likin'
for it.'

A match flared and the lamp was lit. And Edge led his
mount into the building that was a general purpose barn
at this end and a stable at the other. There were three
ploughs, a harrow, a drill and a hoe stored for the winter.
They had been cleaned of mud, sharpened and greased.
Several sets of harness hung on a wall, the leather soaped
and the brass polished. The chains were as free of rust as
the metalwork of the implements. Nearby was an immaculately cared-for cut-under buggy that looked not to have

been used in a long time, and a flatbed wagon, scarred by a great deal of load-carrying but as well maintained as everything else within the barn, which was redolent with grease and oil and saddlesoap and hay and animals.

While Donald Kemp remained at the foot of the stairway that angled across the rear wall to reach the hayloft, Edge took the gelding into the stable section where four stalls were occupied by work horses, one by an animal that was saddle broke and one by a recently milked cow. This left two empty stalls. While the half-breed was bedding down his horse in one of these – taking straw, feed and water from a well-supplied stock – he was aware of the farmer climbing up into the hayloft. When Kemp came down again, he was carrying an earthenware jug, and the knowing grin was re-established on his round, darkly weathered face. His eyes gleamed more brightly in the lamplight as he ran the back of a hand across his moist lips before he offered:

'You want a slug here and now, Mr Edge?' He directed along the barn a wink that a woman would probably have seen as salacious. And his voice was a little slurred – like he had just taken the latest of many drinks today, or maybe it was a very large slug he took up in the hayloft.

'When I'm through here, feller,' the half-breed told him as he finished rubbing down the gelding. Then he took off his hat and coat and rolled his shirtsleeves up to his elbows. Drew a bucket of water from the store butt and set it on the floor. Dropped to his haunches and washed the trail dust from his hands and face without soap. Dried himself off with his kerchief. Came back from out of the far reaches of the lamplight carrying the Stetson, sheepskin coat and damp kerchief. Continued: 'Consider the drink a part of the supper. And I'm in agreement with your wife. If there's the facilities, a man should wash up before he eats.'

Kemp eyed Edge levelly as he handed over the jug and watched him drink – like he was trying to decide if there had been implied criticism in what the stranger had said.

11

This while Edge ignored the farmer, expecting nothing good from the moonshine. But good it was.

'If you make cider as well as you make whiskey, feller,' the half-breed said with a grin of relish, 'then the stink of those rotten apples has to be worth living with.'

The farmer's doubtfulness was immediately allayed by the praise, and his face was suddenly lit by the broadest smile he had yet displayed. 'I ain't never had any complaints from local folks,' he assured. 'You want to try some?'

'Do we have the time?'

'Sure, sure,' Kemp answered, turning away and striding toward the well-preserved and under-used buggy. 'The wife or Annie will give us a call when the food is on the table.' He swung open a door of the rig and Edge heard the clink of glass on glass before the farmer came up with two green-coloured, unlabelled pint bottles. 'Here, enjoy.'

'How many places have you got hooch hidden on the farm, feller?' Edge asked as he set down the jug on a tread of the stairway and accepted the bottle.

Both men unstoppered the bottles and tilted them to their mouths. And after getting a first taste of the cider and finding it as much to his liking as the whiskey, Edge drank as long and with as much relish as Kemp.

'Enjoy it, you did, I figure?' the farmer posed after they had both lowered the bottles with almost half the contents gone. Now his unhandsome face held the expression of a dog with the good deed successfully done, awaiting the well-deserved reward.

'I'd say that what you told me earlier about the cider taking the fire out of the whiskey was pretty close to a lie, feller,' Edge answered evenly. And now he set down the burden of his excess clothing on a stair tread. 'It could just be you wash down this crazy applejuice with the corn liquor?'

Donald Kemp beamed. 'You could be right there, Mr Edge. But I would appreciate it if you will think of what I

12

said as a slight bending of the truth. We Dunkers never lie.'

He advanced to the foot of the stairway and gestured for permission to take a drink of his own whiskey. Edge was midway through sucking some more cider from the bottle and signalled with his free hand for the farmer to go ahead.

'Thank you, Mr Edge.'

'You're a long way from your roots, feller.'

Kemp finished with the jug and handed it to the half-breed. Said: 'The Black Forest of Germany . . . *Schwarzwald*. Yes, it is a long, long way from Texas.'

His Teutonic accent was more pronounced as an expression that threatened maudlin nostalgia nudged the happiness off his face.

'I was thinking of Pennsylvania,' Edge said. 'Ain't that where people of your kind settled when you came from Europe?' He raised the jug and sucked from it.

Kemp watched him with surprise shading into respect, then asked as he accepted the jug back: 'You know of the Church of the Brethren, sir?'

'That's what your religion is called? No, not much. Heard German-American Baptists were called Dunkers. And most of them herded themselves together in Pennsylvania.'

'Ohio, too,' Kemp answered, nodding vigorously. 'Edwina and me and the children, we moved from Pennsylvania to Ohio when my likin' for this and this . . .' he first waved the jug and then the bottle '. . . became a subject of much gossip.' He shrugged. 'In Ohio, it was the same. So we come to the West. To Texas, where we are the only members of the Church of the Brethren for hundreds of miles. Where I am able to be as bad a Dunker as I always have been without offending others of my kind. Except for my wife and my daughter. And they are as true to our faith as always, except only they must worship in private.'

Now he shook his head as violently as he had nodded it

a few minutes before. And took a hurried swallow from the cider bottle which he chased with a hefty slug of whiskey.

'Is running such a neat place some kind of penance, feller?' Edge asked, and lowered his rump on to his sheepskin coat that served as a cushion on the stair tread three from the bottom. He took the proffered jug.

Kemp backed against the wall and slid easily down it until he squatted on his haunches, just an arm's reach away from where the half-breed raised the jug to his lips. The farmer peered intently into the middle distance for a few moments, before he replied: 'Ain't never thought about it that way, Mr Edge. Could be, I guess. Way I see it – way the wife and Annie see it, too, I figure – is that as long as I run the place German-style . . . that's neat and clean and tidy without any goldbrickin' when there's work to be done . . . Well, then I haven't let the liquor get the better of me. Hasn't been spoken of that way between the women and me, but I figure the understandin's there right enough.'

The jug exchanged hands and the half-breed was suddenly perplexed. In his mind a moment ago there had been a question and now, suddenly, he could not recall what it was he had wanted to ask. Next, anger hovered above the rim of confusion: waiting for him to admit he was drunk. Anger at the sandy-haired farmer for providing the liquor. And at himself for drinking so much of it so fast on an empty belly: after several weeks of many days in which he had not taken a drink at all, or had limited himself to a couple of shots of rye or a glass of beer if he happened to be close by a saloon.

Strong drink he enjoyed, but being drunk he hated. Because being drunk was associated in his mind with sickening self-pity born out of grief. Too, it was a dangerous state to be in. For when a man's mind was stewing in alcohol, his thinking process was impaired and his physical responses were drastically slowed. And this could mean for a man like Edge that his life could come to a dead stop.

'Here,' Kemp said to interrupt the half-breed's train of thought.

And as Edge accepted the jug his mind became fuddled with confusion again. The anger that had threatened no longer had even a tentative grip on him as a sensation of warmth and happiness offered itself as an easy alternative to perplexity. He was safe here in the company of this lapsed Baptist who truly placed cleanliness next to Godliness while concocting high-grade liquor and the kind of cider that should only be drunk in shot glasses. And pretty soon the both of them would be summoned to sit down to what would surely turn out to be a fine meal with which to soak up the stuff they were drinking. For if all else about the Kemp place was in such good shape, then the food was hardly likely to fall short.

'. . . name was Kempler when we came over from the old country,' the farmer was saying as he waited, just a little impatiently, for Edge to finish with the jug and pass it back. 'I was Hans and my wife was called Hilda. Anna, she was always as she is called. We change the names when we come to Texas. We take the names to become true Americans. We try never to speak the language of the old country. I do okay at that, you figure?'

'Fine,' Edge agreed, and could not be sure whether Donald Kemp smiled because of the response or because he had retrieved the jug. He tried to take a drink from the cider bottle while he considered the matter, but he had already emptied the whole pint.

The man with the sandy hair and the dull, round face gave him the corn liquor to be going on with. While he hauled himself to his feet with great effort and weaved over to the buggy, leaned inside and straightened up and returned with two fresh pints. Edge lost sight of him behind the uptilted jug for a second or so. And when he saw him again it was in a seemingly much brighter level of light from the single lamp. Too, the farmer appeared to be shrunken in height, but much broader across the shoulders.

15

The half-breed had a question for the man. He was not sure if it was the same one he had lost before. He kept it firmly in mind that he wanted to ask Donald Kemp what had become of the other *children* he had mentioned. But he could not get his lips and tongue to function in unison to voice the query. So he tried to concentrate more deeply by closing his eyes to the garish light and the distorted image of the man. Found he was still unable to utter a word. For awhile, though, what Kemp was saying reached him distinctly.

' . . another before the women call us in to eat, my friend. Here in the barn is the only place I keep a secret stock. Only it ain't really no secret. The wife and Annie both know what's up in the hayloft and in the buggy we don't use no more . . .'

Edge had felt a full bottle of cider press into his free hand and he instinctively clenched a fist as he let the empty one fall. There was just a dull thud rather than a shatter of breaking glass on the hard-packed dirt of the barn floor. The question floated out of his mind. He endeavoured to force open his eyes but had no misgivings when he found out it could not be done. Kemp's tone was shifting toward the maudlin again.

A woman snapped: '*Himmel!*'

Now it was morning and time to pay the price for the night before. The sun was a hundred times brighter than the now doused lamp had seemed to be in those moments before he passed out: and as yet he saw only that amount of sunlight that shafted in through the highly-polished windows of the immaculately kept barn.

He had slept where he had fallen, curled up on the dirt floor at the foot of the stairway. But somebody had placed his hat under his head as a pillow of sorts and tossed the sheepskin coat over his body. But it was inevitable he should wake up cold and stiff-jointed. And he accepted these discomforts as parts of the same punishment that

16

was also comprised of the pounding pain behind his eyes and the taste of hot sand in his mouth.

He reshaped the hat to some extent while he was still on the floor and set it on his head. Then pushed one arm into a sleeve of the coat before he used the stairway to help him get to his feet. When he was fully erect and had his coat on he was able to keep his eyes open and in focus without an accompanying hallucination that his head was going to explode.

He looked around and failed to see Donald Kemp. Also gone was the corn liquor jug and the empty and full cider bottles. His kerchief was draped over a stair tread and he elected to bunch it up and thrust it in a coat pocket rather than don it.

Down at the far end of the barn the horses and milk cow were serenely calm in the bright, cold light of a new day. The smell of the animals was the only taint in the air, until Edge had crossed to the closed double doors. Under these a draught of chill winter air infiltrated, laden with the cloying aroma of the cider apples stored in the out-building across the yard. There was no scent of woodsmoke or cooking food or simmering coffee. So maybe, he reasoned, it was earlier in the day than the brilliance of the sunlight made it seem.

One of the doors swung open as silently and smoothly as last night. And he saw through the skeleton branches of the leafless oak that, in fact, the sun was almost midway up the dome of a patched with cloud south eastern sky. But he saw this only on the periphery of his vision. For the centre of his attention was held by the awesomely inert forms of Donald, Edwina and Anna Kemp. Which hung from one of the stoutest boughs of the tree. Each limply dangling corpse suspended by a short length of rope with the noose knot at the side so that the head was forced into an awkward tilt from the broken neck.

'Did you do that to these people?' a man asked flatly.

Edge's glinting-eyed gaze shifted away from the three

17

dead bodies and his mouthline tightened into a brutal set as he heard the familiar and unmistakable series of metallic sounds that signalled the cocking of a revolver. And his lips hardly moved as he responded through gritted teeth to the uniformed man who levelled an Army Colt .45 at him.

'Don't be crazy, Corporal. If I'd done that, you think I'd still be hanging around, too?'

18

Two

THE NON-COM was in the campaign dress of the 4th United States Cavalry – an out-of-shape black hat with a crossed sabres insignia and a broad brim that sagged under the band, a dark blue tunic cut down from a frock coat, with a yellow kerchief spilling out at the open neck and yellow chevrons on each sleeve, lighter blue pants with a broad yellow stripe down each outside seam and regulation black riding boots with brass spurs. Around his waist was a black belt with a fastened ammunition pouch on the left side and the open holster for the revolver on the right. He did not tote a sabre and although he wore a shoulder belt there was no carbine hung from it.

'I'm supposed to take your word, just like that?' the corporal countered, and there was a note of scorn in his voice now.

'Yeah. And you'd better believe this, too. Once you've put up the pistol, don't ever point a gun at me again unless you plan to kill me. Because I'll sure as hell is hot be doing my damndest to kill you. One warning is all I give.'

Now Edge looked at the man rather than the uniform as the cavalry corporal's face changed expression from a kind of detached melancholy to a challenging scowl. It was the face of a thirty-year-old. On the fringe of handsomeness and with something familiar in the sharpness of the bone structure. He had dark blue eyes that were deep set beneath bushy black eyebrows, a nose that had been

19

broken and re-set slightly off centre and the kind of mouth-line which could not convincingly express a false emotion. Thus, although he sought to generate anger that the half-breed remained so calm in front of the gun, the set of his mouth and a barely discernible tic at one corner revealed he was actually afraid of the situation he had created by drawing the revolver. Then he caught his breath and his six-feet-tall, lithely-built frame became suddenly rigid as Edge stepped out of the barn doorway and growled:

'The women were fixing supper. Kemp and me had a drink of his corn liquor and cider. It's a powerful mix. Last time I slept so long and so deep and so unexpectedly, it was a bullet in the head that caused it. Telling you what happened because I figure you had the right to ask what you did.'

The cavalryman was standing a yard to the left of where Donald Kemp's corpse was suspended. The farmer's feet – one with a carpet slipper still on it – hung at about waist level to the soldier, who tracked the Colt across a short arc to keep the slow moving half-breed covered.

'I'm Harry Kemp. They were my Pa, Ma and sister. I got the right to ask a whole lot more.'

The women were minus their waist aprons but otherwise were dressed as he had last seen them. The soldier's mother was hanging next to his father and his sister was on the other side. Edge halted in front of the older woman and tilted his head to look up the flaccid lengths of all three corpses into the faces with their dead, bulging eyes, bloated by strangulation. For a moment he remained unmoving. Then lifted up his left hand as if to remove his hat as a mark of respect. At the same time, he shot a sidelong glance at the surviving member of the Kemp family. Saw the corporal of cavalry had felt drawn to look up at the death-distorted faces.

Then Edge lunged forward and to the left, so that his left shoulder collided violently with the left thigh of Donald Kemp. Sent the dead farmer's legs swinging toward his son. Harry Kemp uttered a choked cry of horror and staggered backwards, off balance and needing to flail both arms to keep from sprawling to the ground on his back. Edge swerved around the back of the corpse as it swung into an opposite arc. And powered toward the horrified, back-stepping man. In cool control of his own actions, he was able to lengthen a second stride and screw the leading foot around to hook it behind one of the soldier's ankles.

'Bastard!' Kemp shrieked as he began to topple backwards, and knew he was now beyond reversing the motion. But instinctively he continued to flail his arms while he retained his fisted grip around the butt of the Colt. Then he slammed to the ground, spread-eagled and with the breath forced out of him by the impact. And in the second it took him to recover to the point where he could start to plan a countermove, it was too late. The wrist of his gun hand was trapped under the half-breed's left boot. And the pressure was increased as his assailant stooped, drew a revolver and thrust it out at arm's length. Then became unmoving except for the thumbing back of the handgun's hammer after the muzzle had reached to within an inch of the widely-gaping mouth of the helpless man.

'Had a lot of respect for my parents, too,' the half-breed said evenly, the killer glint fading from his slitted eyes to leave his face impassive. 'But I'll make allowances for what happened to your folks and won't take that bastard as an insult to mine.'

Kemp swallowed hard and his mouth worked frantically beneath the threat of the cocked gun. But nothing but the sounds of his ragged breathing came out of his throat.

'Easy, Corporal,' Edge went on. 'It ain't my intention to make you eat crow. Just like for you to keep it in mind for the future: right here and now I could make it so you ate lead. Easy as this.'

He tracked the revolver slightly to the side and squeezed the trigger. Kemp gasped and then clamped his lips together as tightly as he snapped his eyes closed. Was as utterly unmoving as his dead family while the sound of the gunshot echoed between the farm buildings and the dust exploded by the blast and the impacting bullet settled. Some of it on his bristled face – for the hole in the ground was no more than three inches away from his cheek.

When he opened his eyes they were empty of expression for part of a second – like his instincts were taking the time to test the emotional options. Should he be afraid, horrified, angry or gratefully contrite? Then he did a double take at the half-breed, who had straightened up from the stooping attitude and stepped back: his booted foot no longer on Kemp's wrist. And it was bewilderment that flooded his eyes as he recognised the grimace of pain on the face of his captor of a moment ago.

Then Edge began to massage with fingertips the creased skin of his forehead as he explained: 'Case of that hurting me a whole lot more than it did you, Corporal. I have to hope now there's no more occasion for gunfire until this hangover's gone.'

Kemp folded up into a sitting position and pushed his revolver into the holster before he claimed: 'What you told me would have been enough, pal. I know what a gunshot sounds like. Seen what it can do when the bullet hits a –'

'Sure,' Edge cut in as a patch of pure white cloud slid across the face of the sun and the lower level of light acted to dull the sharpness of the pain in his head. 'I brought it on myself. No sweat. You mind if I use the house kitchen to make some coffee? I have my own grounds if there's any hard feelings?'

He had extracted the spent shell-case and reloaded the chamber with a fresh bullet from his belt. Now slid the Colt back in the holster as he watched the cavalryman come to his feet, flexing the muscles of his shoulders and the small of his back.

'I could use a cup myself, pal,' Kemp answered through teeth clenched in a grimace of physical discomfort. Then his features became clouded with grief as he eyed the three

22

hanged forms – the man still swaying slightly after the violence. 'Be in greater need after I've done what I have to about my folks. You help yourself.'

'Obliged,' the half-breed acknowledged, and turned to head for the front of the house, delving into a shirt pocket for the makings. Up on the porch, he paused to glance over his shoulder before stepping through the already open front door. This as Harry Kemp vented a piercing whistle through the thumb and finger of one hand. Which brought a saddled horse galloping down the track from the stage trail, dust exploding from beneath its pumping hooves and drifting out over the fields to either side. Then the cavalryman started toward the barn and the half-breed entered the house.

He had a match ready to strike on the most convenient surface. But as his nostrils filled with the scent of furniture polish, and a moment later he saw how scrupulously clean and tidy the room was, he scraped the match head into flame on the butt of the Colt. Lit the cigarette angled from a side of his mouth and then carried the burnt out match across to the range that was inset into the end wall at the base of the fieldstone chimney. There were still red embers in the ash of the grate. And fresh kindling and some cordwood from a basket in the hearth was blazing in a few minutes, the flames warming the man who had lit the fire and the coffee pot he had set on top of the range.

While he waited, relishing the heat and anticipating the taste that the aroma of coffee promised, he surveyed his surroundings with a bleak gaze. The room was a combined parlour and kitchen and he guessed that two doors in the far wall from the range gave onto a pair of small bedrooms. Which would surely be in keeping with this room: too neat and tidy to his mind, and as spotless as was possible since the women who kept house here had been dead for a number of hours. Furnished for comfort without luxury – with some fine porcelain in a glass-fronted display cabinet and a long-case clock the only items on view that were

23

not essential for day-to-day living between sun-up and sundown for a farmer and his wife and their daughter.

Because the Kemps had been so obsessively concerned with good order in their lives it was plain to see there had been no struggle in this room before they met their deaths. They had eaten supper and the dishes had been done and put away before they went out into the yard to be hanged. The doors to the bedrooms were closed and the family were still fully dressed when they were lynched. There was no sign that anything – valuable or not – had been removed from this room. And it seemed unlikely that something had been taken from either of the bedrooms. If thieves were prompted to kill, they did not hang their victims.

The water in the pot had been bubbling for long enough to make the coffee as strong as he felt he needed it, and so the half-breed abandoned his reflections upon what may have taken place on the Kemp farmstead the previous night. It had been only an academic exercise, anyway. To use up time while he waited for the coffee to be made . . . Or was he seeking an excuse for himself to account for why he had failed to be roused from sleep by the disturbance of three people being put to death?

He grimaced and vented a low grunt as he lifted the pot off the range. There was no excuse. Just the plain and simple truth that it was not sleep that had so detached him from what was happening here last night. He was locked in a stupor from getting falling-down-drunk.

He carried the pot out into the daylight that was still grey, easy on his eyes and the feeling in back of them. And saw that Harry Kemp had been a whole lot busier than he over the past ten minutes or so. Had cut down his parents and sister and eased the nooses from around their necks. From the barn he had brought a burlap wagon cover which he had cut into three pieces. Also some rope. Edwina and Anna Kemp were already wrapped and lashed into their makeshift winding sheets and the grim-faced uniformed man was just about to attend to the corpse of

24

his father as the half-breed stepped down off the house porch.

'The cups in the house only hold a couple of mouthfuls,' Edge said as Kemp looked up, eyes glittering with moisture.

'Ma liked nice things, pal. Never put on the airs and graces. Just liked certain things to be certain ways. Be through pretty soon now.'

Edge set down the pot on the dirt and went into the barn to get the tin mug from his gear at the stable end. When he re-emerged, Harry Kemp was finished for the moment with the corpses and was pouring himself some coffee into an army issue tin mug taken from a bag on his still-saddled cavalry mount. He was dry-eyed now, and there was a streak of dirt across one cheek where he had wiped away some spilled tears with a dusty tunic sleeve. As he filled the half-breed's mug, he posed:

'Told you I'm Harry Kemp, pal?'

'Edge.'

A nod, then a brief chewing of one side of the lower lip. Before: 'I got no hard feelings if you don't, Edge. It was a dumb move, drawing my piece the way I did. But I wasn't in any kind of state for straight thinking. Saw my . . . saw what was hanging from the tree when I reached the start of the track. Too far off to see who they were. But I guess I knew. The way there were three of them. In a daze, I think. Left my mount up there on the trail and came down on foot. Don't ask me why. Saw it was my folks. Saw the door to the house was open. Figured if I was going to be jumped, it would be from in there. Then you showed from in the barn.' He expelled some breath from between pursed lips and shook his head in a gesture of incredulity. 'Well, I tell you, Edge. If you had been Jesus Christ himself along with a band of angels, I'd have drawn my piece. And the way you looked . . .' He shook his head slowly again.

Edge had been carefully sipping the hot, strong,

black-as-tar coffee. Now paused to suck on the cigarette but before he arced it away he replied with a lukewarm grin: 'I guess I still look much the same, but I'm starting to feel a whole lot better.'

'Pa never warned you about the stuff he made having a kick like a whole team of mules?'

'Maybe he did, Corporal. Later, after things got a little hazy. Told me one thing for sure. That doesn't seem to add up with what I'm seeing now.'

'How's that, Edge?'

'Said the family were Dunkers. Way I heard it, that branch of the Baptists is dead set against military service?'

Kemp had been intrigued and ready to be angered by what he had foreseen as a potential criticism of his dead father or himself. Now he was relieved that there was no reason to get mad at the half-breed. 'Guess my folks didn't say too much about me, uh?'

'Nothing, directly. Your Pa made mention of children but there was only your sister around. Never did get to ask him about that. Black sheep?'

'Through and through, Edge.' There was deep sadness on his face again as he looked at the house, the out-buildings and the well-cared-for fields. 'Left this place ten years ago to join the army. Told never to come back. This is the first time I have.'

'Lousy way for a family to break up, feller,' Edge said. 'Even worse, the way you came back to the fold. Much obliged for the coffee.'

He finished most of what was left in the mug and tipped the dregs out on the yard, leaving an elongated dark stain that pointed toward his discarded cigarette butt. And, for just part of a second as he glimpsed the burlap-wrapped corpses, he experienced a twinge of guilt for so wantonly dirtying up the place the Kemps had always kept so neat and tidy. But then, with a brief twist of his lips back from his gritted teeth as he swung to head for the barn, he allowed to himself that nothing was more obscenely dirty than sudden, violent death. And no matter how he looked at it, he had had no hand in this latest orgy of killing.

Down at the stable end of the barn he stripped off above the waist to his longjohns and used a bucket of water from the butt to wash up and shave with the straight razor he kept in the pouch held at the nape of his neck by the circlet of beads. While he was thus engaged, the cow made insistent sounds of distress. For all the noise Harry Kemp created, Edge might well have been alone on the place. He was in process of getting dressed again, feeling cold, but relieved that his hangover now consisted only of a certain fuzziness without pain, when the morose-faced cavalry non-com came into the barn and moved toward the stable end.

'Guess an old farm boy like you can handle milking a cow, feller?' the half-breed asked as he shrugged gratefully into the warm topcoat.

'Sure thing.'

Edge nodded to the stall in which the complaining cow was becoming increasingly restless. 'She's long past her morning time, I figure.'

'You could take care of it, too? If you had a mind?'

Edge was taking his gear down from where it had been hooked outside the chestnut gelding's stall. 'Been out of farming a long time, Corporal. Ain't no part of it appeals to me any more.'

He stepped into the stall and began to coax his mount out.

'Head okay now?' Kemp asked as he went into the empty stall beside that occupied by the lowing and moaning cow.

'Like all I had was a couple of flat sarsaparillas with cold coffee chasers,' the half-breed answered absently, engaged with preparing his horse for riding.

The gunshot, its volume amplified by the confines of the barn, silenced the suffering cow and triggered a chorus of

27

protesting whinnies and snorts from the horses. Edge's head remained fuzzy without pain in response to the report, but the sharp bite of black powder smoke in his nostrils caused a disconcerting stirring sensation deep in his stomach. By the time the chill air of the now much greyer morning had negated the acrid stench of the gunsmoke, all the animals in the barn were silent and calm again.

'Pa taught me how to slaughter stock, too,' Kemp murmured as he pushed the Colt back in his holster and turned from grimacing down at the fresh carcase. 'Got the beast right between the eyes.'

'No sweat, Corporal. With your folks dead, guess it was your cow.' The half-breed made this response as he came upright from stooping to fix the saddle cinch. Now he led the gelding along the barn and out into the yard where the burlap-shrouded corpses still lay in an appropriately neat line beneath the branch of the oak with three short lengths of severed rope tied to it. The noosed ends cut from the necks of the lynch victims were no longer to be seen. Harry Kemp had hitched his horse to one of the white-painted posts that supported the porch roof. The door of the house was now closed. The coffee pot, no longer wisping steam, stood on the dirt of the yard, like the forgotten toy of a sleeping child. The rekindled fire that had boiled the coffee now sent just a faint trace of grey smoke up from the fieldstone chimney into a sky that had the pallor of a fatal illness.

Edge stood beside his horse, the both of them ready to leave – the gelding eager to be gone from the presence of death, but firmly schooled to await the dictates of the man. The man who now took out the makings and without haste rolled and lit a fresh cigarette. Then took out his mug again and poured another coffee. Smoked and drank with impassive lack of outward reaction as he listened to recognisable sounds within the barn. So he saw what he expected after Kemp had opened wide both doors of the barn. And it was the cavalryman who expressed brief, mild surprise before he swung back from the doorway to climb athletically up on to the seat of the flatbed wagon. Two of the farm's quartet of work horses were in the traces and Kemp handled them expertly as he steered the rig out into the open and reined the team to a halt when the flatbed was alongside the corpses.

'I can manage, pal,' the uniformed man announced in the manner of somebody accepting a challenge as he swung smoothly to the ground.

'You have the right to try,' Edge answered, and made another elongated coffee stain across the yard surface. Then stowed the mug and rose into his saddle. Where he waited patiently, conscious of the gelding's eagerness to be gone, while Harry Kemp loaded his dead family aboard the wagon with seemingly effortless ease. When the soldier was done, the corpses were arranged across the wagon bed in as dignified a manner as was possible given the circumstances.

Then Kemp went to bring his army mount from the front of the house and hitched the reins to the rear of the wagon. As he began to unsaddle the piebald gelding, his latent curiosity finally got the better of him. But he elected not to ask the direct question.

'Intend to do more than try, Edge. Intend to see my folks get a decent burial the way God-fearing people deserve. Then intend to see that whoever murdered them gets brought to justice.' He carried his saddle and bedroll to the front of the wagon, heaved it up on to the seat and climbed aboard again to sit beside it. His resolute expression that negated the soft line of his mouth defied the calmly smoking half-breed to take issue with him.

'What about the three horses you left in the barn, Corporal?'

'You want I should slaughter them, too?'

Edge shook his head, almost imperceptibly. 'Seemed

like a waste to cream a cow just because she needed milking.'

'I don't have the time,' Kemp came back bitterly as he took up the reins. Then felt the need to explain: 'The horses have got feed and water enough to last until I get back after taking care of the funeral arrangements.'

Now Edge gave a just discernible nod of satisfaction as he heeled his horse forward; at the same time Kemp released the brake and flicked the reins to start the wagon rolling.

With a tone not so far removed from scorn, the uniformed man growled: 'Blacksmith I served with at Camp Nichols up in the Indian Territory one time, he maintained he liked animals better than people. Like you, I guess?'

'Just claim most animals and most people, Corporal,' Edge replied, and removed his cigarette for a moment so he could spit, and he dropped back to the rear of the rig as they started up the wagon-wide track between the well-husbanded fields. 'Sometimes there are exceptions to prove the rule. Not so very often.'

There was no more talk against the clop of hooves and the rattle of wheelrims until they had reached the top of the track and turned east, toward Pomona. Then, as if the pause of more than three minutes had never happened, Harry Kemp said to the half-breed who moved to ride alongside the wagon seat:

'Guess I was well-disposed to the world in general until this morning, Edge. But when I found my folks that way in the yard, any milk of human kindness in me dried up quicker than spit on a hot stove lid.'

'Can see how what you found soured you, Corporal,' the half-breed allowed.

Kemp snarled: 'You sure it was Pa's hooch that gave you an aching head this morning, pal? And not the effort of trying to crack wise all the time?'

'Head's as fine as my belly now.'

30

'What the hell has your gut to do with it?' Kemp demanded in exasperation.

'After you killed the cow instead of milking her. It started to churn.'

Three

ATER ANOTHER, much longer lull in the conversation, during which Edge seemed comfortably content as he finished smoking the cigarette and Harry Kemp exchanged an impulse to anger for brooding ill-humour, it was the cavalryman who again broke the verbal silence.

'How were my folks, Edge?' His tone was conciliatory but there was latent in his dark blue eyes a warning that he was ready to give as good as he got if the rider at the side of the wagon did not meet him halfway.

'Well disposed toward a passing-by stranger, Corporal,' the half-breed replied evenly as he continued to maintain his easy and habitual surveillance over the country through which he rode. And sensed, without need to closely study the bereaved trooper, the man's relief at receiving a serious and honest answer. Then his eagerness to hear more of the same. 'I reached the place from the rear. For my own reasons I've been riding around any place where people might be for quite a while. Need supplies every now and then. Last night I wasn't ready for the kind of town I'd heard Pomona was. Getting low on a few items. Saw the smoke of a fire from your folk's place and decided to take a look. Friendly night camp would have saved me pitching one. Friendly farmstead could have what I needed to purchase.'

He ensured there was no fire left in the cigarette butt before he dropped it to the trail. And was pensively silent for a few moments, like he was recollecting memories of the previous night – or re-examining his motives for unwittingly getting himself involved in the Kemp family tragedy. Then: 'Figure they saw me from a good way off. Near full night when I was close enough for them to see me in the light from the rear door. I wasn't any sight for sore eyes for the kind of people your folks were, feller. But they didn't let it show too much. Except for your sister. She hardly even tried to give me the kind of welcome your Ma and Pa did. I was invited right off to stay for supper. And they took it amiss when I said I'd feel bound to pay my way.'

Kemp had started to nod, his eagerness at full pitch again after it waned while Edge spoke of his reason for detouring off the lone trail to head for the farmstead. And explained: 'Annie wasn't much for the boys, even when she was through being just a kid. I always figured that was because she was no beauty and none of the boys made any kind of play for her.'

'Your Pa made excuses for her when he showed me into the barn. Then, after I'd taken care of my horse, the drinking got started. I'd say your Pa was anxious for that to happen because he was short on company to drink with usually. Me . . . I guess I had my reason, too – for getting drunk instead of just plain taking a few drinks.' He paused and there was a rueful set to his mouthline which was at odds with the somewhat menacing glint in his slitted eyes as he pondered his motives. Then he vented a low, non-committal grunt and went on: 'Your Pa did most of the talking. Enjoyed it most of the time. Then either your Ma or your sister came to call us for supper, I guess. Which is when I passed out. Yeah, Corporal, I reckon it would be the truth to say your folks were all fine last night. And none of them had any notion of what was going to happen.'

The sky had brightened a little, but there was still no sign of the sun that had been so brilliantly yellow something over an hour ago. The still air had gotten more bitingly cold and had a feel of snow about it. The Wylie Mountains, through which the trail laid an undemanding course, were unspectacular rises of grey and red rock that were mostly flat or round-topped. Here and there fans of black scree spilled down from the high points. The trail was flanked by outcrops of brush – and grass-encircled rock at frequent intervals. Lone leafless trees and small stands of firs were more scarce. The dust of a long time without rain powdered every surface, including the hard packed trail – and showed the watchful Edge that no-one had passed this way on horseback, wagon or foot since the last wind had blown hereabouts. Which meant nothing, he allowed to himself: since there could have been a howling blue norther blowing all night long and he would not have known about it. His constantly-moving eyes and his never entirely dormant instinct for lurking danger signalled that nobody with indifferent or hostile curiosity was watching the slow-rolling wagon and its escorting rider from any of the countless pockets of cover on all sides.

'I appreciate you taking the trouble to tell me about it, Edge,' Harry Kemp said after a lengthy pause, during which he had peered out of his cold-pinched face into the middle distance, his mind crowded with secret thoughts. Then both his tone and his attitude were alert to the present again as he asked: 'You mind telling me something else?'

'What's that?'

'Why you're riding with me?'

'I heard Pomona is a fair size town, feller. Most of its citizens are decent and law-abiding. There's an elected town council and mayor. Sheriff, too.'

'You said back at the farm that it sounded like the kind of town you wanted to steer clear of?'

'The way things were with me yesterday, it was. This morning I need the supplies I wasn't able to get from your folks. Any kind of town with the right kind of store will do now. Since Pomona's the kind of town where the law

34

counts for something, I figure it's best we ride in together. Best for me, anyway.'

Kemp snapped his head around to peer hard at the even-toned half-breed, trying to penetrate the impassive expression beyond which could be latent insinuation. He saw no hint of this, but his own voice was irritably defensive when he claimed:

'I'm convinced you had nothing to do with murdering my folks, pal! If you want to ride on ahead and get your business done in town before I get there, you can trust me not to say anything that's not the truth about –'

'I ain't doubting you, Corporal,' Edge cut in. 'But you said you've been away from this neck of the woods for ten years. I'm a passing-through stranger. Pomona sounds like the kind of town where my kind never make a good first impression. Maybe I'm wrong about it. Maybe I've got less cause to doubt the local citizens than I have to doubt you. Just that I want to be sure that when I leave Pomona I have no reason to do it in a hurry – because the local law figures I fit in with the picture of what a killer is supposed to look like. And the kind of people who are likely to think that way, Corporal . . . Well, I don't guess they'd be likely to pay too much attention to a man who was stopping by again after ten years away from the place?'

Kemp had several times looked to be on the point of wanting to interrupt the half-breed. But in the end he merely gave a rueful nod of agreement. Then felt the need to offer: 'I'm sorry. Ten years is a long time. And I wasn't much more than a kid when I went away. But unless Pomona has changed one hell of a lot, it'll still be much the same kind of town as you've figured it out to be.'

'You didn't pass through it on your way home this morning?' Edge asked as he saw a first sign that they were nearing the town – a layer of smoke from numerous chimneys that hung beneath the low cloud and above a smooth hillcrest. Toward which the trail swung in a gentle curve around a boulder-littered area at the base of a mesa-like slab of sandstone. Slightly north of due east.

'No. Rode in from the other direction. Was on furlough in El Paso. Closest I'd been to home since I enlisted. Occurred to me that it was almost Thanksgiving, and maybe it would be a right occasion to visit and see if my folks had changed their opinion of me.' He breathed a deep sigh. 'Guess I'll never know now.'

'Unless your folks made mention of it to their friends in town, feller,' Edge suggested absently as they crested the rise and were able to see Pomona about a half mile distant across an extensive plateau.

'You said it yourself, pal,' Kemp countered, a little sourly. 'Pa seemed starved of drinking companions. Which didn't surprise me. Ever since they left their own kind back in Ohio they made a point of not making friends. Kept themselves to themselves. Mostly on account of Ma, who I always figured was ashamed of Pa's drinking and how it set them apart from the other Dunkers. Pa went along with her ways because, I figure, he was ashamed of himself. When he wasn't quietly drunk. Anna did what Ma told her. Even thought the way Ma told her. Maybe because she was an ugly duckling girl who never had the chance to do otherwise. I was luckier.'

He glanced at the man riding beside the wagon, and saw Edge had abandoned his all-around surveillance to concentrate his narrow-eyed watch on the community they would soon enter. The half-breed gave no indication that he was listening to what was being told him, and the cavalry corporal discovered himself unconcerned by this. Perhaps he was even relieved that this hard-nosed drifter with the stamp of the gunslinger on him had seemingly not heard the brief tale of woe that summed up the Kemp family history. And now the sole survivor of that family gazed at the town instead of into the past as he switched subject to say:

'It's a little larger than I recall it.'

'Then it probably is,' Edge replied, still pre-occupied.

'To me, anything that stays the same always looks smaller the second time around.'

Pomona was a two-street town that had been established by the Mexicans – or maybe even the Spaniards when the only native born people south of the Rio Grande were Indians. But apart from a few buildings of adobe that still stood, and the crumbled remains of others, Pomona's style of architecture was not distinctly Texas-American.

The main street was three times wider than the trail, the start of it marked by a twenty-feet high pole at either side. Ropes strung up the lengths of the poles revealed that a line of bunting would be stretched across the entrance to the town on special occasions. Beyond the poles, on the north side of the street, there was a row of crumbled adobe buildings with weeds and thorny brush sprouting higher than the collapsed walls. None of the buildings had been very large. Opposite the derelict area was a vacant lot that had once been totally enclosed by an unpainted picket fence. Now just the fence along the street front was intact. At the sides and rear it leaned one way or another or had fallen completely. A heap of stone blocks and some scattered planks of lumber were all that remained of the never-started construction project.

'The old *pueblo* was like that when we first moved out here,' Kemp supplied sardonically. 'Parcel of land across the street was earmarked for a theatre as I recall. I don't remember it was fenced off.'

The main street ran in a straight line for half its near half-mile length, then veered to the left and maintained its generous width. At the point where it angled away from a small stand of stunted pines, a narrower street cut off more sharply to the right. A single story frame schoolhouse was next to the lot where the theatre had never been built and beyond this was a line of two-story, stone and timber houses of medium size that stretched to the mid-town area. Each had enough fenced-off garden space between for building on. But only the school seemed to have been

37

enlarged as Pomona grew. On the other side of the street was a row of smaller houses with no more than an alley separating each from its next-door neighbours. They had no fences at the front and a strip of land out back acted as a communal yard spread with junk. A little over halfway down from the western town limit to where the street turned and another cut off it, there was an adobe church.

When they drew level with it, Edge could see the church had fallen into disuse. And its state of dereliction made the houses of the poor and of the would-be rich appear reasonably well preserved by comparison.

School was out for the midday recess, and many of the house chimneys were contributing to the pall of smoke that the low cloud cover had trapped above the town. The various appetizing fragrances of many meals being cooked were closer than the main body of smoke and so provided the dominant aroma in the cold air: and caused Edge to become uncomfortably aware of the emptiness in his belly. He was conscious, too, of being watched with mild interest from behind some of the windows of the flanking houses. But only as one part of the moving tableau. He was just another stranger coming in off what was surely a well-used stage trail between El Paso and everywhere to the east of Pomona. Of greater interest would be the uniformed trooper who drove a wagon with three burlap-wrapped bundles on the back. Maybe Harry Kemp was recognised. The wagon and team could well be familiar. Also, some of the observers might have sensed that the two men had brought death to town – that the burlap-wrapped freight aboard the flatbed was exactly what they feared it looked like.

'It's not any bigger,' Kemp revised his earlier opinion, and blew warm breath into each cupped hand in turn as he swung his head from side to side. 'Close to like we are, it looks a whole lot more rundown than it used to.'

The street that veered sharply to the south from where the stand of pines was in the crotch of the town's misshapen

Y layout was lined on both sides by adobe buildings. Some houses, stores, other business premises and a church. All were old, crudely constructed and in daily use. There were some people, horses and wagons on the narrow street that had no sidewalks and became a trail some quarter mile or so from the mid-town start.

'They call this Old Pomona,' Kemp explained as he steered the flatbed on to the side street. 'Guess it was all Mexicans who lived here right at the beginning. Just a handful left when I went away. The rest were the poor whites. It doesn't look different in the least bit. Always was on the way to wrack and ruin is how I remember it.'

He reined the team to a halt. And the expression of serene wistfulness that had been a match for his tone of voice was suddenly gone as he peered along the remaining length of the main street that angled toward the north east limit of town. It was replaced by a scowl of disgust and he spoke with bitterness.

'The town undertakers used to have a place down at the end of Old Pomona, Edge. I'll go make arrangements for my folks. The sheriff's office is up there on Main. To the left. If it hasn't been moved. It won't matter to me if you tell first what happened out at the farm. Or if you want to eat or take a hair of the dog, there are a couple of places for that. And the stores most likely to have what you want are –'

Edge had briefly scanned the quiet-at-noontime downtown section of Pomona, and now cut in on Harry Kemp. 'You expecting some trouble, Corporal?'

'Uh?' the trooper grunted as the query penetrated into the private world of resentment that had fleetingly enclosed him. But he had not been so far detached that Edge's words failed to register. He looked at the half-breed and nodded. Was about to augment the response, but somebody else spoke first.

'Hey, ain't you the Kemp kid?'

This from an elderly, wizen-faced woman with grey hair

39

held in a tight bun who had stepped into the doorway of an adobe shack to the right of where the wagon and horseman had halted. There was a single window at the front of the shack, through which could be seen shelves lined with brightly coloured jars. In faded black lettering over the top of the window was the word *CANDY*. The woman's eyesight was bad and she squinted in the sunless brightness of the early winter day.

'Yes, ma'am, Mrs Crabbe,' Kemp confirmed, his tone as polite as the gesture of a hand going up to tip his hat.

'Thought it was you, boy,' the raggedly-dressed old woman replied, her manner as frosty as her opening had been. 'You visited with your family, I'm thinkin'?'

'I was out at the farm, Mrs Crabbe.'

'First time back since you went against your faith and left the place?'

'Yes, ma'am.' He was obviously having to struggle to maintain the respectful attitude toward the coldly unfriendly woman.

'So I'm thinkin' you was told that ain't much has altered in all them years in how Pomona folks think about you Kemps?'

'Depends what you mean by trouble, pal,' the cavalry non-com said tautly in delayed reply to the half-breed's query. This as he tipped his hat to Mrs Crabbe and flicked the reins to start the rig rolling again. Then, peering back over his shoulder to keep the squinting old woman in sight, he raised his voice far louder than was necessary to tell her – and all others within a long range of earshot: 'I never got the chance to find out if my family would even talk to me! Because all three of them had been murdered!'

There would have been a body of sound throughout Pomona of which the turning of the flatbed's wheels and the clop of hooves formed only parts. But all those other contributing sounds were now only noticeable because of their absence as Kemp drove the wagon and Edge rode

40

his horse through a town that for stretched seconds was in the grip of a fragile silence.

'Holy Mother of God!' Mrs Crabbe suddenly blurted, and squinted hard at the bundles on the back of the wagon as she made the sign of the cross.

And then the whole town was buzzing with talk as the news was broadcast from one end to the other. While, signalled by the same harshly-announced revelation, the level of interest in the newcomers to Pomona was abruptly intensified: none of it surreptitious anymore. People pressed their faces to windows or came into and out of doorways to stare with a whole gamut of emotions at the trooper, the half-breed and the burlap-wrapped corpses. Morbid curiosity and vicarious horror. Sadness and not quite hidden satisfaction. Pity and sympathy. With, here and there, indifference and impassiveness.

Because they struck an out-of-context note in their surroundings of the one time Mexican quarter of the now largely Texas-American town, Edge took particular note of two morose-faced Indians who had emerged from a shack across the street from the tiny church. He also found himself strongly conscious of the elderly priest who stood like an inanimate statue in the arched doorway beneath the belltower of the time and weather ravaged church. The thin-framed, hollow-eyed man in a grubby cleric's collar and much darned cassock made no gesture to acknowledge the presence of recent death – except when his impassiveness was momentarily gone and was replaced by a slight movement of his mouthline that seemed to express a sense of fulfilment.

'The Comanches are new to me, Edge,' Kemp rasped, and there was a tautness in his voice that indicated the effort he was having to make to keep his anger in check, while the people of Pomona revealed their initial reactions to the triple killings. 'Father O'Donnell never had any time for anyone who wasn't a Catholic. Doesn't drink anything stronger than communion wine and figures all who do are damned. You can guess what he thought of us because of Pa making such fine cider and corn liquor?'

'From what I saw of the way you gave those two sad-sack braves the evil eye, Corporal,' Edge replied evenly, 'I'd guess you think a whole lot less of Indians than the priest does of drunks who have no time for the Pope?'

'You haven't guessed wrong, pal!' Kemp said through pursed lips, and followed the sour-voiced comment with a stream of saliva that hit the street surface as he reined in the team. 'And that's just not on account of I've lost a lot of good friends to those sneaky, heathen, uncivilised bastards in the time I've been wearing this uniform.'

He wound the reins around the brake lever and swung down to the ground in front of the last building on the right hand side of Old Pomona, before it became the open trail that curved into a patch of broken, brush-cloaked terrain three or four hundred yards due south. The building had started out as a small adobe shack but then, several years ago, a frame extension had been added on at the rear. This went back a short way and then to the side for a greater distance to form an *L*-shape. The adobe was white, patched with yellow, and the timbered section of the building was a dried-out grey. Just as the Comanches had seemed misplaced, so did a square brass plate that was screwed to the centre of the closed door at eye level. It had been assiduously polished over a lot of years, until the engraved legend was now barely readable. But when Harry Kemp stepped back after hammering the end of a fist on the door, the still-mounted Edge was able to discern the inscription: *OTIS BOONE – FUNERALS*.

'Mr Boone came to Pomona from one of the big cities back east,' the trooper said after watching the half-breed decipher the long-service sign. 'Brought that with him.'

He used his fist on the door again.

'Closed for lunch!' a croaky voice called from just beyond the doorway. And then came the sound of a bolt being slid home.

42

'Is that to everybody, Mr Boone?' Kemp countered with just a faint trace of strain in his tone. 'Or just me and my dead?'

He and Edge both shot glances back along the street. Horses stood stock still in their traces or at hitching rails, and the two Comanches watched the scene out front of the funeral parlour with the same inactive glumness as they had shown before. Outside of this, the street was lifeless. And here, and along Main Street, the sounds of a town idling through the noontime break of a working day again provided an unobtrusive backdrop to the unwelcome disturbance caused by Harry Kemp.

'Heard what you told Blanche Crabbe about your family being killed, sir!' Otis Boone answered and his attempt to sound deferential made his voice even croakier than before. 'Murder is the law's business first, Mr Kemp. I am unable to do anything until Sheriff England has dealt with the deceased. We'll be open again this afternoon and perhaps by then the sheriff –'

Edge had slid from the saddle and moved across to stand beside Kemp. His light blue eyes glittered with unconcealed cold determination, while the dark blue ones of the trooper emanated the kind of frustration that might signal an impending explosion of white-hot rage.

'You really want this feller Boone to take care of burying your family, Corporal?' the half-breed asked. His voice was not loud but it had a quality of insistence upon being heard that caused the mortician to break off what he was saying.

'Want the bodies put in caskets, Edge,' Kemp answered. 'Mr Boone used to be the only undertaker for miles around. Still is, I guess. He makes fine caskets. I'll take care of the burying. That'll be out at the farm.'

'You'll have to see the sheriff first, sir,' Boone insisted again. 'Then if he says it's all right, I'll open up and –'

Edge lifted his right foot off the ground and leaned back from the waist as he powered it into a forward kick that

43

sent the heel of his boot smashing into the door above the latch. The door burst inwards and the startled mortician vented a horrified cry as he sprang backwards. The door crashed against the inner wall.

'You're open already, feller,' the half-breed said evenly to the short and fat, round-eyed and treble-chinned man of about forty who stared across the threshold at him.

'You're not Otis Boone,' Kemp accused.

'Otis Boone Junior!' the fat little man in the shiny and threadbare dark suit rebutted, struggling to recover his composure. 'It would have been my father you knew in the past. I came to Pomona to take over the business when he passed on several years ago.'

Talking helped him. Along with keeping his hands busy smoothing down his thinning dark hair and brushing lint off his jacket sleeves. It also allowed time for the two Comanches to stroll down the street. These braves, who were in their mid-twenties, were attired in a mixture of store-bought and native clothing – moccasins and Stetsons, buckskin shirts and denim pants, beadworked waistcoats and long dusters. They now looked menacingly sullen instead of moodily ill-humoured.

'You as good as your Pa was at the job?' Harry Kemp asked, apparently unaware of the slowly approaching Comanches, who withdrew their hands from the deep pockets of the dusters as they came near. Their hands were clenched into tight fists, signalling that the braves were prepared to back up mere mean looks with vicious action. 'I'm not in the market for anything as fancy as that, though.'

The trooper nodded to indicate the room in back of the undertaker where a highly polished black casket with glinting silver handles stood on a table.

'That is a sample of my finest work,' Boone responded quickly and there was just a hint of pride in his manner. 'I'll be pleased to meet whatever requirements you have, once permission is granted for me to –'

44

'You getting trouble from these men, Otis Boone?' the slightly taller of the two braves asked.

'You want Black Hawk and White Eagle to lend a hand, Otis Boone?' the other added.

Kemp, who was closest to where the two Comanches had come to a halt, showed he had been aware of their advance down the street. He was coldly unsurprised and did no more than glance scornfully at them before he commanded: 'Get the hell away from me before I do something you scum will regret.'

Both Indians growled a terse comment in their native language. The tone of their voices and the hardening of the menace in their eyes conveyed the obscenity of what they had rasped at the cavalryman.

Kemp tensed to whirl and face the threatened attack. Edge halted his move to take the makings out of a shirt pocket. Boone stepped up into the doorway and said with an implied threat in back of new-found confidence:

'I think the gentlemen now understand my position?' He looked pointedly at the Comanches and then quizzically at Kemp and Edge.

'A dollar each, Otis Boone,' the taller brave said.

'You die cheap, even for scum,' the trooper growled, and started to turn.

The half-breed began to swing in the same direction. But kept his narrow-eyed gaze fixed upon the suddenly nervously frowning face of Boone as he drawled: 'You got three customers already, feller. Ain't exactly a slow day. You don't have to drum up business this way.'

The undertaker's Adam's apple bobbed a number of times. Some saliva spilled out of a corner of his mouth.

'Talk does not frighten us, Otis Boone,' the shorter Comanche assured the white man who was afraid. 'You will pay a dollar apiece?'

'No!' Boone snapped. 'All right, Mr Kemp! I'll take care of the remains. Face up to the consequences of dealing with the law later. To avoid unpleasantness now.'

Morose again, and muttering bitterly in their own language, the Comanches swung into an about-face and ambled back up the street: hands deep in their pockets once more.

'Wise decision, pal,' Kemp said as he moved toward the wagon.

'I had no real choice,' the undertaker complained and stepped away from the threshold of his premises to help the trooper with the corpses.

'Had you on the ropes, feller,' Edge said as he climbed into the saddle of the chestnut gelding. Gestured toward the burlap-wrapped corpses. 'It was either fight us or box them.'

Four

EDGE RODE his horse out of Old Pomona, and rounded the
stand of timber to start up that stretch of Main Street
that angled toward the north east. He was headed for a
two-story building at the far end on the right, which had
a sign on the roof that proclaimed it was The Black Hat
Hotel and Saloon. But he was not so intent upon reaching
this objective that he failed to take note of other aspects
of his surroundings.

For most of its length, this stretch of Main had buildings
only on the left. A bakery, then a meat market. A general
store and next to this a feed and grain supplier. Then came
a meeting hall with a freshly-painted cardboard sign fixed
across the front: *ALL INVITED TO THE THANKS-
GIVING SUPPER THURSDAY NEXT.* The thought of
turkey with all the trimmings made Edge even more disconcertingly aware of how hungry he was. But this was not why
he elected to ride on by the law office that was between the
meeting hall and the stage line depot. Harry Kemp had his
own problems with the people of this town, which had to
include the sheriff. It was only right the soldier who had
returned to such grief should have the first opportunity to
put his case. If that created troublesome repercussions for
the half-breed . . .? Well, he would then owe nobody anything hereabouts and he was well experienced in handling
his own troubles in his own ways in such circumstances.

Beyond the stage line depot was the livery stable, then

a clothing store, a boarding house and a barber shop. Most of the buildings were of frame construction, single story with roofed sidewalks two steps up from the street surface.

On the less developed side of the street, there was a small park area beyond the clump of stunted pines: an expanse of well-trodden grass with as many bare patches as there were purpose-made flowerbeds – forlornly short of living plants at this time of year. Here and there, evergreen shrubs continued to thrive, emphasising the absence of healthy colour over most of the lawn. Four well crafted but long neglected benches formed a square at the centre of the park, facing away from a concrete plinth on which stood a red rusted cannon. Nobody was sitting on the benches in the biting cold of this late November early afternoon. Just as nobody else was moving on the entire length of Main Street as Edge rode toward the far end. Passing a Protestant church on the other side of the small park from the pines. Then a cemetery. Next a weed-choked vacant lot across which the graveyard had ample room to spread. Finally reached the hotel, where he dismounted and hitched his reins to the rail which ran for half the length of the porched front of the brick and timber built place.

There were no other animals at the rail. No sounds of a saloon doing any kind of business emerged from the batwinged entrance of the balconied building that was stamped with the same kind of intangible but indelible mark as everything else in Pomona – the people included. Pomona was a community that had once been prosperous and proud. But the promises on which it had been founded had been unfulfilled. And hopes had turned sour. It was a failed town, not too many steps removed from becoming a ghost town.

Edge paused to light the cigarette he had rolled during the slow ride from the funeral parlour. Then went up the three steps and across the porch, booted feet rapping hollowly on the boards. The batwings creaked on dry hinges. Then he was treading on sound-muting carpet that had taken a lot of wear over a great many years.

'Mister, am I glad to see you,' a man greeted effusively.

Edge moved toward the bar counter which had one man behind it and another in front. It was the customer, smiling broadly, who extended the greeting.

'Why's that, feller?' the half-breed responded as he scanned his surroundings fleetingly.

'Because maybe you can help me out?'

Edge bellied up to the bar, several feet down from where the other customer stood, and answered: 'No sweat. The doorway is right back there.'

'Hot damn, you know I wasn't meanin' that!'

The bartender spread his previously grim-set features with a grin far brighter than the one that was now gone from the scowling face of the would-be panhandler. This as he moved hurriedly along the counter to where Edge stood. He wiped the already clean bartop with a towel fixed to his waist apron, and invited: 'What can I get you?'

'You serve chow here?'

The bartender was of medium height and build with a thin, clean-shaven face that lacked character and was slow to show the signs of getting older. He could pass for early twenties at first glance. He was maybe almost twice this. He had a mop of jet-black hair and his eyes were almost as dark, set in stark white surrounds – which maybe meant he did not indulge in his stock in trade. Above the leather waist apron he wore a faded grey shirt and a bootlace tie. He replied:

'Not as a general rule these days.'

'But general rules can be broke the same as any other kind?' Edge suggested.

'Broke is sure as hell what I am, mister,' the other customer complained, and peered balefully into the empty glass on the counter before him: like this and not his thirst for what it had once contained was responsible for its emptiness.

49

'I got to eat, too,' the bartender acknowledged. 'Guess I can toss some more of the makings into the pot and stretch it over two. Take awhile?'

'Been hungry longer. But it'll be awhile yet before my belly hits my backbone.'

'Drink to help pass the time?'

'A shot glass and leave the bottle. Rye. For the cold.'

The bartender supplied what was requested and apologised: 'Ain't worth my while firin' up both stoves these days. Unless some special occasion gets the Black Hat filled up. Slight chance anyone else comes in and wants servin', give me a call?'

He emerged from the far end of the bar counter that ran along the rear wall of the saloon, which was wider than it was deep. And went through a doorway in an alcove beneath the broad staircase that swept through a gentle curve across the end wall. The stairs were guarded by an elaborately-carved banister that matched the style of the counter and the dozen tables and accompanying chairs that were spread about the room with generous space between them. The frame of the massive mirror that was angled between the ceiling and wall above the counter was carved and stained to the same pattern. Similarly the frames of the cow country oil paintings that hung on the whitewashed walls.

Like the carpet he trod to get to the ornately cast stove that did have a fire in it, the furniture and decorations of the Black Hat Saloon had seen better days. And, in keeping with the town outside the batwings, there was about the place an admission of the inevitable: that the good times would never be repeated.

'You're the man that rode in along with Harry Kemp and his dead folks, ain't you?'

The stove that generated such welcome warmth was close to the other end of the saloon from the stairway. Edge sat down at a table on the open grate side of it, in the chair that placed his back toward a blank corner. As he uncorked the half-full bottle of whiskey he needed to turn his head just a little to look at his sole fellow customer. Who was beyond fifty, a once overweight and now skinny man whose flaccid skin fitted his frame as badly as his stained and patched blue denim coveralls. He had the bloodshot eyes of a drunk and the nut-brown skin colour of an outdoor man. Because of the way the fleshless skin sagged down from the bone structure, his face had the lachrymose look of an old bloodhound. He did not sound too drunk, and wouldn't have looked that way had he not leaned so heavily against the counter.

'Right, feller,' Edge told him as he poured a drink and removed the cigarette from his mouth to take a sip.

'Casey's my name, mister. William Casey. Everyone calls me Willy.'

'I ain't one to go with the crowd,' Edge countered, and gave a nod of satisfaction after the rye had hit his stomach without causing any unpleasant reaction because it was otherwise empty. But he took just another small sip before he set the glass down and replaced the cigarette. It would take longer for the rye to get into his bloodstream that was still run with Donald Kemp's booze.

'You get to sample any of the stuff that was made out at the Kemp place, mister?' Casey asked. 'Meanin' no disrespect to Joe Sinclair here at the Black Hat . . . But the stuff he sells just don't stand no comparison with that corn liquor the Kemps made.'

'You holding that opinion, it means you didn't kill them, I guess,' Edge said, taking off his hat and feeling warm enough to unfasten the sheepskin coat.

'Me?' Casey exclaimed, disconcerted. 'Me string up the Kemps? The way I am? With this useless chunk of dead meat I gotta drag along with me for the rest of my natural?'

Mortification had changed to a brand of defensive anger as he spluttered an explanation for his innocence. And then he demonstrated that it was not the effects of drinking that made him need the bar counter to keep him on his

51

feet. For as he pushed himself away from it, he unhooked an unfancy walking cane from a pocket of his coveralls on the blind side of Edge. And thudded it viciously against the calf of an obviously dead leg before he used it to support himself now he had turned from the counter.

'Case proved, feller,' Edge allowed and saw the fires die in the bloodshot eyes.

'Damn right, mister.'

'News travels fast in this town.'

'Same as in all small towns, mister. And the way that Harry Kemp yelled the way he did to Blanche Crabbe at the candy store . . . Well, maybe everyone in the whole of west Texas knows it already.'

'I was meaning the news that got here to the saloon from the Boone funeral parlour ahead of me.'

'Uh?'

'The corporal yelled out that his folks had been murdered. Guess Otis Boone knows by now they were hanged. And you just said something about them being strung up, didn't you?'

'That was how it was done, uh?' the lame man said pensively. And shook his head slowly as he went on: 'If you say I said it, I ain't gonna dispute that, mister. But it was just a manner of speakin'. Most would have said the same thing, I'm thinkin'. On account of for a lot of years, most Pomona people have been sayin' that stringin' up is what the Kemps needed.'

'You still need helping out?'

Even when he smiled broadly in keen anticipation of an unexpected pleasure to come, Willy Casey's face suggested he was only a moment away from the depths of misery. 'You mean with a drink?'

'Usually I am. But right now I'm ready to be generous.'

Casey remembered to pick up his long-empty glass from the bar counter before he started to weave between the fine furniture to reach the table where Edge sat. He used the cane with the skill of experience to move with awkward but painless speed. But then he paused after jerking the chair out from under the table across from the half-breed. And it was apprehension one step away from melancholy that altered the slack lines of his face when he warned:

'I ain't gonna say nothin' I don't know to be the honest truth, mister.'

Edge nodded and countered as he pushed the bottle to the centre of the table: 'If I find out you've lied after drinking my whiskey, Willy, you won't even have the one leg left to stand on.'

Casey found himself fleetingly trapped by the steady gaze that was directed up at him by the glinting threads of ice blue between the almost cracked-closed lids. And he licked his lips out of a sense of fear rather than because he needed a drink. Then he broke free with a sideways jerk of his head, as if there had been a palpable link between his eyes and those of the half-breed that needed to be violently snapped.

'Look!' he said sharply, and this time he was momentarily held by something that had captured his interest out front of the Black Hat Saloon. 'There goes Cloris Snellin' down to visit the grave of her little girl again.'

Edge glanced out through the window to the left of the batwinged entrance. Toward which Casey had gestured with his hand clutched around his glass. And was in time to see a woman reach the foot of the steep set of steps that came down from the Rio Grande Boarding House diagonally across the street. A short, stout woman dressed in a black coat buttoned to the throat and almost reaching the ground, black gloves and a black hat with a fine mesh veil which completely concealed her face.

'Has something to do with the trouble between the Kemps and this town?' the half-breed asked as the woman attired in mourning went out of sight of the saloon window, moving with an air of inexorable determination to get where she was headed, no matter what hindrances might be in her path.

53

'You don't know nothin' about any of it?' Casey asked, surprised, as he lowered himself on to the chair and rested his cane across his thighs. He asked with a hand gesture if he was free to help himself to a drink and Edge nodded that he was.

'The idea is for you to tell me what I don't know, Willy.'

'But I don't know who you are,' he countered as he filled his shot glass.

'Name's Edge.'

'Or why it is you want to know –'

He broke off with a startled cry and leaned hard back in his chair when Edge folded forward. But there was just latent menace in the half-breed's move – which he completed by swinging to the side and taking the cigarette from his mouth to toss in the grate of the stove. When he settled comfortably back in his chair again, he took another sip of rye and offered evenly:

'If you want to go try bum some liquor off somebody else, Willy, feel free. I ain't in so much hurry to get the information.'

'The Kemps were Dunkers,' Casey blurted. 'That's a bunch of religious people that are kinda like the Quakers and the Amish. Against bearin' arms and fightin'. You heard of them kind of religions, Mr Edge?'

'Sure, Willy. You have that shot now, and pour yourself another.'

'Appreciate it,' the sad-faced man responded, and accepted the invitation. And in the time this took he was able to modulate his voice back to normal. 'When the Kemps first came to Pomona – must be close to twenty years ago, I'd say – what their religion was didn't make no difference to nobody around here. Except for James O'Donnell who's the Catholic priest and Alvin Webster who takes care of them of the Episcopalian persuasion. But what the hell, that don't make no never mind, does it? Donald and Edwina Kemp set up in the farming business out on the El Paso Trail. Along with young

Anna and Harry. Did real well at it. Kept themselves to themselves and mostly we only ever saw them when they brought in their produce to supply the local stores. Always the finest available. Them Kemps sure knew how to raise first-rate crops. No corn liquor nor cider way back then. Nobody even knew they were makin' it. Guess everyone figures they was tee-total. Them bein' so religious.'

He broke off to take another drink. But this time he thought he saw a warning glint in the narrowed eyes of the man across the table. And he put down the glass still half full.

'Then came the Injun trouble. A bunch of renegades – Apaches and a couple of Arapaho – started to hit some places around here. Off to the east and north where most of the farmsteads and small ranches are. War between the States was on then, and there weren't too many able bodied fightin' men left around here. Most were off doin' what they could for the Cause. Donald Kemp, he was as young and healthy as anybody. But he just out and out refused to ride with the Injun-fightin' militia that Ralph Lasky got together.'

He pointedly avoided looking at Edge as he picked up the half-full glass and emptied it at a quick swallow. Then ran the back of a hand across his slack mouth before he continued:

'Ralph's been the big man around here for a long time. Used to be the banker when the town needed one. Now he owns a lot of the best real estate in Pomona. Been elected mayor for six or seven years.'

'Banker still, except he calls himself a loan agent these days,' Joe Sinclair put in as he appeared at the doorway beneath the stairs. And remained there, his bleak expression perhaps serving a dual purpose: to display his feelings about the lack of business and his opinion of the town mayor. 'Food'll be with you in fifteen minutes or so.'

'Fine,' Edge said, and returned his attention to Casey. Who hurriedly withdrew the hand that had been inching toward the bottle. 'The Indians raise much hell, feller?'

'Nah. Scared a lot of folks. Stole some stock. Set fire to a couple of barns. We killed two of them and winged a few more and that was enough to send them runnin' for the hills. Somebody got an arrow in the arm, as I recall.'

'Eddie Morrison,' Sinclair reminded him flatly. 'The day they hit your place and you took the lead in your leg that crippled you, Willy.'

'So, what?' Casey snarled with a grimace, directing a resentful stare over the length of the saloon at the bartender. 'The man wants to hear about the Kemps' troubles. Not mine.'

'Have a drink, Willy,' Edge invited.

The day darkened as Casey's impulse to anger subsided. He glanced toward the batwinged doorway and the two uncurtained windows at either side, through which the dull light of the grey day spilled. Said: 'Looked like snow. Don't no more. I appreciate the offer, Mr Edge. Accept it in payment for what I'm sayin' to you. If I took it on account of pity, I'd most likely gag on it.'

The half-breed nodded, as into his mind raced a stream of painful memories that stretched back over many years. Those from the most distant past triggered by Willy Casey's mention of the Civil War. Of more recent origin were the events that had been his reason for the long, lonesome ride that he voluntarily ended at the Kemp place. The cause, too, of failing to check the drinking jag in the barn when he knew he was getting helplessly drunk.

'Figure there ain't even a heeltap of pity left inside me,' he said, his tone taut with brittle hardness as countless images flashed across the forefront of his mind in less than a second. Starting with Jamie Hedges. And Beth Day, before she became his wife. Then the girl named Conchita who was responsible for him riding yet another aimless trail toward somebody else's violent trouble. 'All been used up on my own account.'

Casey nodded in much the same manner as the half-breed had done. But there was a danger he could dwell in an embittered past for much longer. 'Know the feelin' well, Mr Edge. Pretty soon after I got the dead leg, my wife run off with the hand I hired to take care of the heavy chores on the ranch. Tried to keep the place goin' for awhile with a whole string of drifters that breezed in and out of this neck of the woods. Finished up with them two no-account, bone-idle Comanches that nowadays live on Old Pomona and cheat the townspeople outta high pay for lousy work.'

The hissing sound of liquid spilling on to hot metal caused Joe Sinclair to whirl out of the doorway and hurry back to the kitchen. It also intruded into Casey's train of thought. And now he shook his head more vigorously, irritated with himself.

'And *I* told *him* it wasn't me you wanted to hear about,' he growled as he poured himself a third drink. He shrugged. 'But it's almost all told now, anyway. For a time the Kemps were treated like they had the Black Death or somethin'. Wouldn't nobody have any dealin's with them. But it didn't seem to bother them none since, like I told you, they'd always kept themselves to themselves. And as for makin' a livin', they just started to take their crops to El Paso. Further to go, but didn't bother them none on that score, neither. Gradual like, Pomona folks started to do business with the Kemps again. They'd stop by the farm to buy. And soon enough was doin' that so it hit the local merchants. Which was when they started in to trade again with the Kemps like before.'

Sinclair returned from the kitchen carrying two china plates heaped high with steaming food. As he set one of these down before Edge, he announced: 'Just a mess of hash, mister. A little beef. Mostly it's vegetable.'

'I'm obliged,' the half-breed said, extracting the spoon from where it had been thrust into the side of the heap of food.

57

'Enjoy,' the bartender invited and carried his own plate behind the counter.

'Course, country people's memories are long, Mr Edge,' Casey went on. 'Never forgave what they never forgot, most of them. Me, I did. Folks that don't believe in bearin' arms . . . Well, that's their right.'

'Especially when those folks make good liquor and sell it cheap, Willy,' Sinclair contributed without rancour.

Edge ate the food that was lacking in the flavour his palate would have appreciated. But it had the bulk his stomach demanded.

'Can't be denied,' Casey allowed easily. 'It was when folks started to deal direct with the Kemps out at the farm that their sideline in corn liquor and cider came to light. Can't be denied, either, that I ain't the only man who takes a drink that looked more favourably on the Kemps after samplin' . . .'

He let the contention remain unfinished as the clop of hooves and rattle of a wagon rose in volume on the street. And all three men in the saloon looked toward the windows as Harry Kemp steered the flatbed through a tight turn and halted it immediately out front of the Black Hat Saloon. In place of the three burlap-wrapped bundles that had previously been the rig's freight there were now the same number of unadorned pine funeral caskets.

'Lousy homecoming for him,' Sinclair said with feeling, his youthful face aged by a frown. And he set down his spoon like he had suddenly lost his appetite.

'Ought never to have happened,' Casey growled solemnly, and finished at a swallow the third drink that had remained untouched for so long. 'Not just on account of what a family don't do because of its religious persuasion.'

Edge started in to eat the food faster as he saw the depth of determination on the face and in the manner of the trooper who climbed down off the wagon and advanced to the threshold of the saloon.

'The local lawman is going to investigate the murder of my family, pal,' Kemp said as he halted in the entrance, a white-knuckled hand hooked over each half-open batwing. 'Be best if you came back out to the farm with us, I reckon.'

'Why's that, Corporal?' the half-breed replied with a mouthful of food.

'The sheriff's open minded. But he's new around here. A bunch of local people have already made up their minds it was a passing through drifter who did the killings. If you try to leave Pomona –'

'I get the drift,' Edge cut in, and scraped up a final spoonful of food before he rose from the chair. He took a thin roll of bills from his pocket and peeled off one, which he dropped to the table as he looked at the bartender to ask: 'A buck cover the chow and what's gone from the bottle?'

'You got some change due,' Sinclair said dolefully as he continued to gaze out of a window of his place at the coffins.

'Maybe I'll collect in cash or kind when I'm back through here,' Edge said as he put his hat on.

'Feel free,' the youthful looking, close to middle-aged man offered as the departing half-breed approached the batwings, which were still creaking as they swung after Harry Kemp had turned away from them.

'I plan on staying that way,' Edge drawled as he left the relatively warm atmosphere of the saloon and moved out into the cold air of a November afternoon. Added as he looked down this stretch of Main Street: 'This just ain't the kind of town I find in any way arresting.'

Five

HARRY KEMP was already back up on the seat of the wagon. Midway down the street on the right a man sat on a horse. This was out front of the law office. On the sidewalk close by, a small group of men were engaged in low-voiced but apparently intent argument with the one astride the horse.

'Neither the sheriff nor me are saying you have to come, Edge,' Kemp pointed out after he had watched the half-breed unhitch the gelding from the Black Hat rail and swing up into the saddle. 'If you want to take off on your own when we're out of town – or now – won't be any skin off our noses. I believe what you told me and Larry England goes along with how I feel.'

'I told you, Corporal,' Edge said evenly as he backed the gelding away from the rail and tugged on the reins to head him in the same direction as the wagon. 'If I look behind me when I'm out of this town I don't want it to be because somebody's coming after me.'

'You hear anything in the saloon?' Kemp asked as he set the wagon rolling.

'About some Indian trouble that goes back a lot of years. You'd have been just a kid then.'

'Sure. But I remember it,' the uniformed man answered.

Then, by mutual consent, the exchange between the wagon driver and the accompanying rider was ended. This as the chorus of low-voiced but embittered talk directed from the sidewalk toward another mounted man faltered and died away: just before Edge and Harry Kemp would have come within earshot of what was being said. All eyes showed a keen interest in the half-breed. None more so than those of the lawman.

They were coal-black eyes, widely set beneath craggy brows and the dominant features of a square-cut face that was deeply burnished and extensively networked by the lines of life. The amount of grey in the hair that showed under his hat brim and in the straggly moustache that almost hid his broad mouth was emphasised by the element-darkened coloration of his skin. It was the face of a man close to fifty – on which side it was not possible to determine. A pleasant, rather than a handsome face, with an old and badly healed knife scar on the right side of the jaw. England was at least as tall as Edge, but he carried a lot more weight. Most of the excess looked to be fat, and most of it had been put on since he bought the grey frockcoat that was in danger of popping the buttons that fastened it from neck to waist.

'You're Edge,' the Pomona sheriff greeted tersely, his lived-in face not altering from the hard set with which he had listened to the caustic arguments given him by the group of men on the sidewalk. 'I'm Sheriff Lawrence England. Glad you agreed to come along. Kemp told me of your part in this business. I always like to deal direct with a witness in the investigation of a crime, though. Hearsay isn't –'

'No sweat, feller.'

'As peace officer here in Pomona, stranger, Larry England is answerable to the town council!' a business-suited, derby-hatted little fat man snapped, his manner impatient and his face wearing a dark scowl of irritability. 'He was elected to the office of sheriff by a free vote of all citizens who bothered to vote. But he can be removed from his appointment by a majority decision of the town council!'

Edge said: 'Figure he knows that.'

61

'He sure enough does,' a man wearing a white waist apron growled. 'Just been –'

Edge broke in: 'Can't figure why I should give a shit about how you Pomona people hire and fire your lawman.'

None of the half dozen men grouped on the roofed sidewalk out front of the law office had been viewing the half-breed with any degree of warmth in back of their overt scrutiny. Now all of them scowled in open animosity, although the attempt by Otis Boone to match the ill-feeling of the others was undermined by the nervous way he kept blinking and dry-washing his soft, pudgy hands.

'Your manner does not cause me surprise,' the spokesman of the group said in a brittle tone. And his grey eyes, filled with contempt, expressed without need of further words his opinion of the half-breed as a type of man he felt he knew well. 'I simply wish to give you fair warning, stranger. The badge that Larry England is wearing could well carry no weight if he refuses to obey the instructions of those who pay his keep. Of course, I cannot foresee what the decision of the town council meeting will be, but –'

All the men on the sidewalk, who with the exception of Boone were in the same sixtyish age group as the one doing the talking, kept bobbing their heads in automatic agreement with what was being said. Then all of them froze, and were abruptly as anxious as the many-chinned undertaker when Edge broke in, his tone as ice cold as his glinting gaze:

'You're Ralph Lasky?'

The little fat man quickly recovered his composure and confirmed: 'That is correct, stranger.'

'The mayor?'

'You know that, I feel sure.'

'A piece of horse sense for you, feller. Next time you threaten me, the mayor better have a Colt to back him up.'

62

There were some gasps and noisy gulps as Edge made to heel his mount forward.

'He's got one here and now, saddle-tramp!' a tall, skinny man with a liver-spotted face spat out. His right hand was already in a pocket of his duster and he did not start to withdraw it until he had spoken his piece.

'Don't be a crazy old fool, Jake!' England snarled. And wheeled his bay gelding so that his bulky body was between the oldest man on the sidewalk and Edge.

'Sheriff's right!' Lasky agreed, his tone and his expression showing a greater degree of anger than England as he half turned to glower at the old-timer, with a revolver butt visible in the fisted hand he now thrust back into the deep pocket.

'All right, all right!' Jake growled sullenly, and silenced a rising volume of rasping talk that had started to sound within the stores down the street from the meeting hall beyond the law office. 'But the more I see and hear of this tough talkin' stranger, the more I'm certain he done for the Kemps. So you men better not make me sheriff after Larry's been fired. Not if you don't want me –'

'Shut up, you stupid old fool!' a woman who sounded as old as Jake yelled from one of the stores.

'Let's go,' England instructed with a glance at Edge and Harry Kemp, and they complied – the half-breed and the lawman riding side by side ahead of the team in the wagon traces.

There was more talk within the stores, and as the trio of men rode by, each of them could sense watching eyes following their progress from the feed and grain suppliers, the general store, the meat market and the bakery. Maybe the surreptitious watchers were harbouring a wide range of emotions, but the men subjected to their scrutiny were aware only of animosity.

The mourning-garbed Cloris Snelling did not remain out of sight. She emerged from the church between the cemetery and the town park and paused to glance through the concealing veil at the wagon as it trundled along the centre of the street. Then she moved toward the gateway in the cemetery wall, nothing in her carriage supplying a clue to what her facial expression might be behind the veil.

When the angle of Main Street had been turned and they were heading due west between the once fine houses on the left and the line of little more than shacks on the right, England vented a long sigh. But this was not sufficient to expel all the heat of his pent-up anger. And he directed a stream of saliva at the hard-packed dirt of the street. Only then did he feel able to relax the strained set of his face without fear of a scowl spreading involuntarily across his features. Instead, he merely looked wearily in need of a good night's sleep.

'Guess there isn't a local ordinance against spitting in the street, Sheriff?' Edge said, delving for the makings as England took out a plug of chewing tobacco and bit off a chunk.

He gazed directly ahead and chewed some juice out of the tobacco for several seconds before he answered: 'Lasky and his bunch aren't in any need of an excuse to get rid of me, Edge. They don't need an excuse to do anything they want in Pomona.'

'But it doesn't bother him, pal,' Harry Kemp put in.

England pushed the tobacco into one ballooned cheek and spat again. Dark brown this time. And he scored a direct hit on an upright post between two sagging stretches of the fence at the front of the site for a once-planned theatre. Then he cleaned off his lower lip and the bushy moustache that hid the top one with the back of a hand and said:

'It's not my town. Been here close to a year and a half. It was just going to be a stop on the way to California. There was a little trouble. A couple of tough-talking kids who wouldn't have stepped on a bug if they were sober rode into town after visiting with the Kemps. Tried to stick up old Jake and Rose Driscoll at their general store. I got the drop on them, smacked them around a little and ran them out of town.'

They were out on the open trail beyond the rope-hung poles, and Edge did a surreptitious double-take at the lawman as he blew out some smoke after lighting the fresh rolled cigarette. Realised he had been wrong: Larry England was still mad inside at what was happening in Pomona. A simple sigh and a spit had not been enough, and he was now using even-toned talk as a safety valve through which an almost undetectable pressure of high tension was escaping.

'Happened in the afternoon that followed the morning that Pomona buried its old lawman,' England continued. 'And I mean old. I figure he was pushing eighty when he cashed in of old age. I was in no hurry to get to California and the living's been pretty good and easy since a handful of Pomona people voted me into office. Wasn't anybody stood against me, but that never made me take the job any less seriously.'

He fell silent and, riding alongside him, Edge was able to see with a quick glance that Larry England had talked his way back from the threat of an explosion of rage that he knew would have been futile now that he was removed from those responsible for needling him. From the wagon seat, the cavalry non-com was only able to see the uncommunicative backs of the two riders out in front of the wagon team. And his tone revealed a harsh lack of concern with any interests other than his own when he accused:

'I guess nothing this serious ever happened since you got your nice and easy job in town, pal?'

Until he realised that Edge had now turned his head to watch him, the lawman's face was starting to twist into a glower of anger again. And if England had allowed himself to be the victim of this rising rage for a second more, Edge thought, it was likely he would have needed a violent outlet to expunge such a depth of feeling. But, under the cool-eyed, faintly challenging surveillance of the half-breed, the lawman was able to get a grip on his self control after just one more spit of tobacco-stained saliva at the ground. Which splashed to the side of the trail as they reached the lip of the plateau on which Pomona was sited.

'That's right, Kemp,' the sheriff said flatly. And when he looked back over his shoulder as they started down the sloping curve of the trail, his deeply weather-stained and time-lined features expressed nothing more than weary resignation to whatever kind of dirty-ended stick life was going to hand him on this occasion. 'But I'm the only law there is around here right now. If you want to wait until the Pomona citizens appoint a new man to the job –'

The trooper was an intelligent and a perceptive man who suddenly sensed the kind of dangerous emotional terrain into which he had wandered. And perhaps he also realised he was out-numbered two to one in terms of affinity. He pulled a face to show self-deprecation as he cut in: 'Hell, I'm sorry. I'm way out of line. If you were that kind of lawman you'd still be back in your warm office and your job wouldn't be up for grabs.'

England nodded acceptance of the apology and then made much the same kind of allowance as Edge earlier in the day. 'You just this morning found your whole family wiped out. Guess you're bound to have trouble thinking straight for awhile.'

Probably the afternoon had not gotten any colder and the west Texas air had been as bone-chilling in town as it was out in the open country. But it felt a whole lot colder to Edge as they moved down to the foot of the easy slope and started on the curve that swung around the mesa of sandstone with the clutter of crumbled rocks along its base. The sky looked greyer and lower and the light was murky. Perhaps there was a smell of rain in the air and this had actually lowered the temperature, he reflected as he turned up the collar of his sheepskin coat so that it brushed the underside of his hat brim.

England began to blow into his cupped hands at frequent

intervals while Kemp, who wore no topcoat over his tunic, seemed unconcerned by the weather: although his off-centre nose and the cheeks that flanked it were blue-veined.

'Pomona people aren't really such a bad bunch,' the sheriff said suddenly to end a lengthy pause. He got rid of the chewed-out wad of tobacco. 'You saw them at their worst and it's my guess it was all bluff and bluster.'

'You ain't just talking to kill the time, feller?' Edge invited and pinched the embers out of the cigarette butt before he flicked it away.

'Kemp's right. Nothing this serious ever happened around here since I was appointed to my job. And nothing as bad for a lot longer than that, is my guess. They didn't know how to face up to it and they handled it wrong.'

'You reckon they'll see the error of their ways and let you keep your job, pal?' the cavalryman asked, his tone sardonic rather than contemptuous.

'Maybe,' England answered evenly. 'But that's not what bothers me.' He blew into his hands once more and looked at the half-breed. 'The town councillors were real eager to have me arrest you, Edge. Just because you were out at the Kemp place when it happened. And because you fit in with their idea of what a killer could look like.'

Edge showed him a mirthless smile that was colder than the air temperature as he responded: 'They're not the first bunch of people to hold that opinion of me.'

England nodded. 'Okay. But in this case it wouldn't go no further. Even if you went back to town now and Lasky and his crew tossed you behind bars, they wouldn't hold you for trial unless they had some real hard evidence you were guilty. Okay, they'd kick me out of my job for not going along with their opinions. They're small-minded, small town people that way. But they're decent and law-abiding and God-fearing. They wouldn't railroad a man they knew to be innocent.'

'But they have to know I'm innocent, Sheriff,' the

half-breed said tautly. 'And I figure I'm going to have to prove that myself.'

'I reckon so,' the lawman agreed regretfully. 'Don't know too many people in Pomona – and none on the town council – who'll pay any attention to what I say when I've been fired.'

'And there's no doubt that I've inherited the grudge those Pomona people have held against my family all these years,' Kemp added. 'So I reckon nobody'll even stand still long enough to listen to anything I have to say.'

'That's the reason why I'm back-tracking on this trail,' Edge said with a glance at the man riding beside him and another over his shoulder at the one driving the wagon. 'Not that I don't trust you fellers to do your best to see justice is done. What I don't trust are usually decent and law-abiding people who have something more than God to fear.'

'Right, pal!' Harry Kemp snarled. 'Especially the kind of people that can carry a grudge for so long as that bunch.'

He jerked a thumb over his shoulder in a vicious gesture that was a match for the look on his face. England seemed about to speak again in defence of the town and its citizens for whom he had worked without trouble for a year and a half. But although he recognised that Edge was likely to listen with equanimity – or more probably with indifference – he suspected that the cavalry non-com was poised on the verge of explosive anger. So in both instances he would be wasting his breath.

Once more there was just the combination of sounds made by the wagon and horses to disturb the otherwise utter silence that hung in the bitterly cold atmosphere pressed between the low clouds and the unprepossessing landscape of the Wylie Mountains. And the trio of men remained mute for longer than before. For ten minutes or more. Each watching their surroundings with varying degrees of detachment. Until two spurts of smoke acted to draw their attention to one spot.

Then Edge reined in his horse, Kemp brought the wagon to a sudden halt and England snapped:

'We got company.'

The two rifle shots cracked out so close together they sounded almost as one: the bullets fired from an area of high, broken ground two hundred yards along the trail on the left. Both bullets kicked up divots of dusty dirt, wide of the stalled group. But a second later England's horse went down onto the knees of its forelegs as two more spurts of muzzle smoke again pinpointed the positions of the sharpshooters. The bay's cry of pain and the snorts of alarm by the other horses almost drowned out the rifle reports this time.

'Oh, my God!' the lawman bellowed. And it was an entreaty rather than a mild blasphemy. As he kicked free of his stirrups and hurled himself out of the saddle: fleetingly unworried about the bushwhackers while he concentrated all his efforts on plunging clear of his crashing horse.

Kemp jammed on the brakes of the wagon and threw himself off the seat. Purposely sprawled out full length so that he was able to power himself into a roll beneath the rig as a part of the same smooth series of actions. He drew his revolver.

Edge leapt from his saddle, the Winchester clear of the boot before his trailing leg had swung over the gelding's rump. And the rifle was cocked, aimed from the shoulder, before he hit the ground: sure footed and evenly balanced.

England had not moved since he sprawled to the trail after the plunge off his falling mount.

Two more puffs of black powder smoke showed against the broken ground ahead and to the left. The half-breed's horse reared. Two rifle shots sounded. One of the team horses dropped in an instant without a sound of pain. Then a revolver was fired. Edge went down on one knee as his horse became four footed again. Dust billowed and was gritty. But the acrid gunsmoke stung the eyes more painfully as Kemp followed up his opening shot with five more and Edge triggered as many with the rifle.

The uniformed man had to take care to fire between the stamping legs of the surviving team horse as the animal struggled in panic to drag the brake-locked wheels of the wagon. But with a revolver over such a range he knew he was firing only for effect. The half-breed exploded his shots just as deliberately as he by turns squeezed the trigger and pumped the lever action of the repeater. It was not his intention to fire for effect: and the killer grin that drew back his thin lips from clenched teeth and cracked his eyes to the narrowest of glinting ice-blue threads signalled the kind of pleasure it would give him to see the ambushers slumped in bullet-riddled, blood-splattered death among the rocks that were their cover.

It was not to be.

There had been just the six shots fired down at the wagon and its two-man mounted escort. And afterwards there was no sign of movement up among the rocks when the muzzle smoke had drifted away and vanished. Then the hammer of the Army Colt clicked hollowly against the base of an empty shellcase. A sixth expended cartridge thudded to the ground after it was ejected from the Winchester. For several stretched seconds the horses of the ambushed party were subdued. Then others, at a distance up the trail, were urged into an instant gallop.

Edge rose to his full height and Kemp scrambled out from beneath the wagon and got to his feet. England remained face down on the ground, silent and unmoving.

The half-breed's horse, one of those in the traces of the wagon and the cavalry mount hitched to the rear were restlessly uneasy in the aftermath of sudden violence: and now made enough nervous noise to mask the diminishing thud of galloping hooves until the sharpshooters had ridden out of earshot anyway.

The team horse that had been shot was dead from a bullet in the head. The lawman's bay gelding was sprawled out on his side, exhausted by several doomed attempts to regain his feet. A massive amount of blood had gushed from a chest wound and now the flow was reduced to a trickle. The animal whimpered pitifully and its upward facing eye constantly rolled around in the socket – like the horse was searching desperately for a source of salvation from pain and fear: or something to blame for the distress that had left him so pathetically helpless. Edge reached the stricken animal in three strides and put him out of his misery with a single shot to the head. Sloped the rifle to his shoulder.

In isolation the report sounded many times louder than the recent barrage of gunfire. The dead horse spasmed for several seconds and then was still and awesomely silent. The other animals were eerily calm in the wake of the killing of one of their own kind.

The half-breed's face was impassive as he peered toward the rocky area from which the ambush had been sprung. Kemp moved across the trail to drop to his haunches beside the spread-eagled sheriff. Asked anxiously:

'You all right?'

'Just winded, I think,' England rasped through gritted teeth as he accepted the cavalryman's help to roll over on to his back. He gently kneaded the base of his belly with both hands. 'Unless you can see any blood?'

'No, there's no blood.'

The Pomona sheriff took a series of deep breaths and then again readily accepted help as he rose gingerly to his feet. Said tautly: 'Thanks. Sprawled out in the open like I was, I figured the best idea was to stay down and play dead.' He grimaced toward the carcase of his horse, then tried for a wan smile as he added: 'It worked. You think I'm the England there'll always be?'

'Maybe,' Edge replied evenly as he pushed a final reload through the loading gate of the Winchester and thrust the rifle back in the boot. 'With a moustache like that it's hard to see if you've got a stiff upper lip.'

Now a scowl swept the never-secure smile off the lived-in face of the lawman as he snapped: 'If you're saying I was scared stiff, you –'

'Hey, I'm sure he didn't mean nothing like that, pal!' Harry Kemp growled. 'Right, Edge?'

The half-breed had hunkered down and was starting to unfasten the harness from the dead team horse. He looked up, head turned to gaze with hard-set eyes at where the uniformed man had stepped in front of the glowering Larry England. He drawled: 'It was just his horse I put down.'

Six

ONLY ESSENTIAL words were exchanged while the three of them shared the chores of hauling the dead animals off the trail and putting the cavalry mount in the traces. England was sullenly silent, obviously resentfully certain that Edge considered him a coward. Kemp was having trouble curbing his impatience to get rolling. The half-breed's lack of expression and unhurried attitude combined to present a true reflection of his innermost feelings.

When they were on the move again, the lawman riding as a passenger on the wagon seat beside the corporal, and the half-breed sitting his saddle directly alongside the two of them, the still ill-humoured England asked caustically:

'Doesn't it bother you, Edge? The way we were bushwhacked?'

Kemp was less agitated now they were rolling. He shifted his quizzical gaze away from the rocky high ground where the ambushers had been hidden, and shared an apprehensive look between the Pomona sheriff and the mounted man. He said in a hard tone: 'Hey now, we've got enough trouble without stirring up more between ourselves!'

'Always bothers me when guns are fired in my direction, feller,' Edge replied, and dug out the makings without interrupting his seemingly casual survey of the terrain on all sides.

'You sure as hell don't show it!'

'You didn't see his face when he was blasting away

73

with the rifle, pal!' Kemp blurted. The retort came out instinctively and even before he was through speaking his expression showed he regretted giving in to the impulse.

'Damn it, Kemp!' England exploded. 'You think the same way he does? You think I was too scared to move back there when –'

'I'll tell you what I think,' Edge broke in evenly on the angry tirade. And both men on the wagon seat swung their heads to peer at him – the lawman with eyes blazing toward a higher pitch of anger and the corporal expressing a tacit plea that Edge should not needle England further. 'I think that smoke over to the south west is rising from your folk's place, feller.'

He hung the freshly-rolled cigarette at the corner of his mouth as he finished. Then pushed the unlit match back in a pocket and took a firmer grip on the reins as he thudded in his heels to demand an immediate gallop from the gelding. Heard both the surprised men yell, but was unable to discern what either said as the thudding of fast-moving hooves and the clattering of the suddenly-speeding wagon filled the cold air.

The air in the immediate vicinity of the Kemp farmstead was not cold as Edge neared the end of a gallop of more than half a mile flat out. At first he had spotted just a few tell-tale wisps of black smoke against the grey sky. But as he raced closer to the hollow in which the Kemp farmstead was sited the smoke thickened. Swirling upwards in a turmoil from its blazing source. But then becoming less turbulent as it made contact with the low cloud ceiling and spread out into a massive and less dense pall.

As he angled off the trail and kept the gelding at the same headlong gallop across the sloping fields that had been so scrupulously farmed by a now dead farmer, Edge saw that the house and both out-buildings were burning fiercely. With yellow, blue and red tongues of flame showing through the smoke that billowed out of open doorways and most of the shattered windows.

Then, from out of the doorway of the barn there came something with more substance than flame and smoke. It was a horse, bolting from the sight and sound and stink of burning. It would not be able to outrun the pain of being scorched. The animal swerved into a tight turn to gallop clear of the other two blazing buildings. Came off the yard and for several seconds stayed on a collision course with Edge's tiring mount. But then the loose animal saw the gelding with a man in the saddle and veered away. And whether by instinct or coincidence he headed toward the far corner of the Kemp property where two other horses were standing: tails flicking, heads tossing and sweat lathered flanks trembling. And it was only now that the half-breed saw them, and recognised by their markings that they were the pair of Clydesdales that had also been occupants of the stable end of the barn.

He slowed the gelding then, and the animal needed little encouragement to make a snorting halt: breathing raggedly, both from weariness after the gallop and apprehension at being so close to the crackling flames and swirling smoke. For a few moments after the horse had come to a standstill, the half-breed remained in the saddle: a hand close to the jutting stock of the booted Winchester while his slitted eyes raked the farmstead for a sign of the arsonists. But until the wagon slid to a skidding stop up on the trail and Kemp and England lunged off and came running across the sloping fields, there was nobody else to be seen.

Both men were yelling, but again Edge was unable to discern what they said. This as he swung off his mount, gave the gelding a reassuring stroke down his nose, and began to move toward the burning buildings. He did not hurry, so it was not long before the running men breathlessly overhauled him. The taller, older, more heavily built Larry England was relieved to be able to slow and match the pace of the half-breed. But Harry Kemp went running on by, roaring a stream of obscenities that were soon masked by distance, the failing power of his punished lungs and the angry cacophony of the raging flames as they consumed the contents and fabric of the house and out-buildings.

'You see anyone?' the Pomona sheriff gasped.

Edge breathed in deeply of the hot, smoke-reeking air as he and England moved up alongside Kemp: at a point on the track several feet short of the yard where the barrage of heat was starting to make itself felt to an uncomfortable degree.

'Kerosene,' the scowling cavalry corporal rasped.

'With some of your Pa's corn liquor to help it along,' Edge added. Then: 'No, Sheriff. Those horses up the hill there were the only living things still around when I got here.'

Both England and Kemp only now became aware of the three still fire-spooked horses up at the north west corner of the property. And they peered toward the small group of animals for a long time: welcoming the pause that allowed them to catch their breath – and maybe to collect their thoughts.

'The well over between the house and stable is the only water?' the lawman asked after awhile. He sounded deeply weary.

'Yeah,' Kemp confirmed and his tone was bitter. 'The bastards.'

England bit off a chew of tobacco and Edge lit the cigarette that had been angled at the side of his mouth since he began to race to the fire. Another aroma, not so unpleasant as many of the others, began to emanate from one of the burning buildings. And when England detected it he expressed puzzlement.

'Roast beef,' Edge supplied.

'It was long dead before it started to cook,' Kemp added. Then said again, with less aggressiveness: 'The bastards.'

Then, as the three men continued to wait and watch – unable to penetrate the scorching barrier of heat to get to the well in the far corner of the yard – a new sound was heard. Just as the fragrance of burning meat had come only from one out-building, so the shattering of exploding bottles came from the other. Sometimes a hissing effect followed the crash of breaking glass. Sometimes there was a low-toned roar. Depending upon whether cider evaporated in a second to steam or if high proof liquor provided aromatic fuel for the voracious flames.

'Stringing my folks up from the old oak wasn't enough for those small-minded, small town, decent and law-abiding Pomona people,' Kemp said, his tone cold and even now, after a period of several seconds during which countless bottles were shatteringly heat-exploded in a chain reaction that drowned out all other sounds of the inferno. 'They had to burn the farm, too.'

'Now, Kemp, you can't accuse the whole town of this,' England warned grimly. 'It was just a couple of sharpshooters who stalled us out on the trail.'

Edge was temporarily detached from the sights and sounds and smells of this fire. And he turned his back on the burning buildings: only then was able to force into the dark recesses of his mind an image of another blazing farmstead. A memory that had come from many years ago . . . Many miles away . . . Iowa . . .

'I'm not saying everyone who lives in that lousy town came out here and struck a match,' Kemp countered in the same, strangely menacing, icily calm manner. And he looked defiantly at England and Edge: like he was eager to be given an argument to provide an outlet for his dangerously pent-up feelings.

But the lawman seemed tongue-tied as he chewed the wad of tobacco and stared fixedly at the flames and smoke – which were suddenly driven skywards with new impetus as the house roof caved in. Kemp would have been drawn to jerk his head around and peer in the same direction by the violent sound: but something about Edge's manner caused him to do a double take at the half-breed. Then to shift his curious gaze up at the trail where Edge was looking.

The three horses that had broken out of the barn were still up there, calmer now as they foraged on an area of grass beyond the trees that marked the property line. But it was not these animals that held Edge's deadpan attention. Instead, two others and the wagon they were hauling and the man who drove the rig that moved at a leisurely pace along the trail from the west. The horses were a fine pair of big greys and the wagon to which they were attached by highly-polished, brass-decorated harness had probably been built to haul dry goods. But that was not its present use. It was an enclosed rig, with a long window in the side panel hung with white lace curtains and black drapes. The body was painted bright crimson, the sides of the wheelrims were green and the spokes were blue. Either the garishly colourful wagon was brand new or it had only recently been refurbished, for even in the dull light of a winter mid-afternoon the paintwork gleamed.

The driving seat was recessed into the body with just the footboard and a matching length of the roof projecting at the front. Thus, only the lower legs and the hands and forearms of the driver could be clearly seen by all three men who now watched the unhurried progress of the distinctive wagon on the trail. There was a small, circular window for the driver to see out from the side of his seat but the distance and angle did not allow the trio down in the hollow more than a glimpse of movement rather than form through it.

'Will you look at that?' England muttered.

'It's damn hard not to,' Kemp replied with a slow shake of his head. 'Who the hell would drive a vehicle like that?'

'Somebody who wants to be noticed, I guess,' Edge offered.

'Hey, someone's riding in the back!' the lawman rasped as the black drape was pulled aside and let fall again quickly, to fleetingly show a face at the window just before the wagon was steered into a turn. Off the trail and onto the track that cut between the fields to lead down to the burning buildings.

There was no change in the measured pace of the wagon as it came down into the hollow, and the driver appeared to be totally incurious about the fire and the trio of men who watched him approach. Until England finished unbuttoning his frock coat and jerked it apart – to reveal the five-pointed silver star pinned to the left side of his vest, and allow him clear access to the holstered Remington on the right side of his gunbelt. Then the wagon was brought to an immediate halt, and the driver did not need to raise his voice very much for his complaint to carry over the sixty or so yards.

'Hell, Sheriff! Was just fixin' to lend a hand! If you and your buddies ain't in any need, I'll just turn this thing around and head on back for the trail!'

He was a dude. A tall, powerfully built man of around forty dressed in a city-style three-piece suit of light blue and a caped ulster coat of light grey that he wore draped over his shoulders, the sleeves hanging emptily at the sides. Around his neck was a white silk cravat, and a derby hat the same shade of grey as the topcoat was set at an angle on his head. His shoes were white and highly polished.

His face was more in keeping with his voice than his garb – rough-hewn and weathered to a dark tan that emphasised the clean whiteness of his teeth. It was a square shape, clear-eyed and with an easy-to-smile mouth, of a type that might suggest at first glance a man of dull wits and inherent honesty.

But even if the half-breed, the cavalry corporal and the lawman were naturally of a trustful disposition in normal circumstances, none of them was in a state of mind to take anyone or anything at face value.

'You didn't exactly come running, stranger,' England pointed out, and let go of the flaps of his coat. 'Know for a fact this smoke can be seen from a real long way off.'

'Hell, it could've been comin' from a timber fire, Sheriff. Or somebody could've been burnin' a heap of garbage. A whole heap of reasons for the smoke, could've been. And none of them any business of mine. Then, when I seen what it was burnin', I seen too that you three men weren't exactly rushin' around to put out the flames. So there didn't seem no need for me to –'

'Who are your passengers, feller?' Edge cut in on garrulous dude.

'Was about to say, mister. There looked to me like there wasn't no need for me to give Miss Molly and Miss Brenda no hell for leather, bumpity-bump ride down to here.' He thudded the side of a big fist on the panel behind the seat and yelled: 'Hell, girls, come on out and say hello. Ain't nothin' to be afeared of: not with the law and the army around.'

He swung smoothly down from the seat as a door was heard to open at the rear of the wagon. Then a set of steps was dropped into place below, and the women emerged from the brightly coloured rig and came around to the side. A blonde and a brunette. Each of them thirty or so. The blonde no taller than five feet with a full-blown figure. The brunette close to a foot taller and skinny thin. Both wore elaborately styled gowns predominantly coloured the same as the wagon's body, and more suitable to a city's ballroom than a west Texas farm. The blonde's was tight-fitting above the waist so that it blatantly displayed her generous curves. The brunette's was nowhere tight, probably to camouflage her lack of prominent curves. The shorter and fleshier woman had a brand of doll-like prettiness. The other one emanated a greater degree of sexuality. Both of them moved with the hip-swaying gait that underscored the advertising message transmitted by their provocative smiles.

When they had sidled up to flank the tough-looking, talkative dude and adopted the time-honoured seductive stance – a hip thrust sideways with a hand resting on it –

England spat a stream of tobacco juice down between his own splayed feet and growled:

'Hey, they're whores.'

'Hell, that's right, Sheriff!' the dude countered effusively. And broadened his grin as he reached out with both hands, first to pat the rear of the blonde and then the brunette. Introduced: 'This here is Brenda and this one's Molly. Me, I'm Jim Bishop.'

'Sonofabitch,' Kemp said softly. And was again in the grip of the strange icy calmness that had injected tension into the fire-heated atmosphere before the luridly painted wagon showed on the trail.

Molly suddenly made haste to get a handkerchief from where it was stowed up the short sleeve of her dress. Just got it to her face as the sneeze exploded.

Edge said: 'Bless you.'

'Thanks,' she responded thickly and blew her nose. 'Just can't shake off this damn cold in the head.' She sniffed wetly as she replaced the handkerchief up her sleeve and, almost like an automaton resumed the hand on hip attitude and spread the alluring smile back on her over-painted face.

'Me, I take care of these lovely ladies,' Bishop hurried on after his veneer of good humour had momentarily cracked when the brunette introduced the mundane side issue of a head cold into his sales pitch. 'Make sure no harm comes to them while they take care of the customers.'

'I just don't believe this,' Kemp said, rocking his head slowly from side to side. His dark blue eyes seemed suddenly to be fired up by a fury that he was incapable of venting.

'Hell, I ain't suggestin' . . .' Bishop said quickly as he recognised that England and Kemp were starting to recover from the surprise that had controlled their responses until now. 'Look, I don't know nothin' about all this fire and how you people are connected with the place. Whatever, there ain't no question that me and the girls expected to do business right here and now. Hell, no!'

Molly sneezed again. And this time it came so unexpectedly fast she had no chance to get the handkerchief. She sniffed and used the back of a hand. Brenda expressed disgust and Bishop's face showed hard-eyed anger for a half second before he forced his rugged features into the shape of an earnest frown as he went on:

'We came to help.'

'We don't need any, pal!' Kemp rasped. 'This is my place as of this morning when I found my folks strung up from that tree there.' He jerked a thumb over his shoulder. 'When we can get to the well, the fire'll be almost out. Nothing left to save.'

'Holy cow,' Brenda gasped.

Molly sneezed, blew her nose and sniffed.

Bishop looked sick to his stomach. Offered: 'Hell, what can somebody say?'

'Try goodbye, pal. Then get yourself and your no-good women off my property. Plan on burying my folks here as soon as the fire's out. They were deeply religious. I wouldn't want to know there were whores like those and a man like you anywhere around when I –'

The dude's face had darkened with anger again. And although the women were tacitly pleading with him to let it be, it was plain the man was readying himself to snarl a rebuttal at Kemp as soon as the corporal was through. And it was equally clear that the cavalryman was dangerously close to unleashing a more violent fury in the direction of Bishop and the women. Until Edge cut in on the non-com before he could finish. He said evenly:

'He's had a rough day, feller. We're all making allowances for that.'

'That's right,' England augmented quickly, anxiously switching his gaze between Kemp and the dude.

'I think we oughta go, Jim,' Brenda urged nervously.

Molly tugged at one of the loose hanging sleeves of the ulster coat. And this meant Bishop could give vent to his

82

anger at a less volatile target than Kemp. He snatched the coat sleeve out of the whore's hand and snarled:

'Leave go, you snotnosed bitch!'

When she cowered back from him, expecting to be hit in the face with more than just the spittle of his rage, he found himself able to get a tenuous grip on his composure. And his expression and voice were placating as he shifted his attention to the three men with their backs to the diminishing fire.

'Hell, I can understand what kind of day he's had. I'll just take myself and my girls away like the soldier wants. Tell you, though, that we plan to stopover in Pomona for tonight. Maybe for a few days if there's good business to be done in town. I know this here ain't the time nor the place to –'

'I only once had any truck with a whore, pal,' Kemp broke in as Bishop turned from between the women to climb up on to the wagon seat. 'When I first left home to enlist a long time ago. Caught the clap off her.'

Bishop and both women were poised to snap indignant counter claims at Harry Kemp who seemed to be using even-toned talk as a safety outlet for the final dregs of his earlier unstable rage. This time it was England who made his point first, to check the others.

'And there's an ordinance against prostitution in Pomona,' he warned.

Bishop dropped onto the seat and gestured with a jerk of his head for the women to get back aboard the brightly-coloured rig. But Brenda stopped and attempted a seductive glance over her shoulder as she asked of the half-breed:

'How about you, bud? You have any rules about whores?'

'No, lady. Just about women in general. Like mine to have less meat on them.'

'Up your ass, creep!' she snarled. She made haste to climb the steps and enter the rear of the wagon.

'So maybe I'm more your type, uh?' Molly suggested thickly, and used the back of a hand to brush the wetness away from her nose again – which interrupted her smile of enjoyment at Brenda's rejection.

Edge tipped his hat and re-lit the cigarette that had gone out while this farmstead fire acted to bring to the forefront of his mind the harsh memory of seeing the Hedges' farm after it was put to the torch so many years ago.

'Never go with a woman who has a runny nose, ma'am.'

'A cold is all you'll catch off me, mister!' she snapped.

'I've always figured it could mean she's full right up.'

84

Seven

BISHOP STEERED the multi-coloured wagon into a tight turn and headed it up the gentle incline of the track between the fields to the trail. And the watching men could see that the lower half of the door in the crimson-painted rear panel of the rig was decorated in a green and blue chequerboard pattern. The upper section was cut with a window, hung with the same kind of white lace curtains and black drapes as the side windows.

'A bordello on wheels,' Harry Kemp growled. 'That really is the craziest thing I think I've ever seen.'

When she felt it was safe to do so, after the wagon was more than halfway back to the trail, Brenda pulled aside the curtain and drape at the door window and made a face.

'They're going to find themselves in trouble if they try to set up shop in town,' England muttered as he began to re-fasten the buttons of his frockcoat.

'It'll fall to the new sheriff to run them out of Pomona,' the cavalryman pointed out.

'God, that's right,' England said, a little surprised. And there was a look of regret in his coal-black eyes as he toyed with his bushy moustache.

Edge glanced at the house and its two out-buildings and discovered that what was left of them now brought no unwelcome images from the distant past into his mind. There was no force in the flames now, and the smoke was predominantly grey instead of black – and it spiralled lazily rather than billowed up toward the disintegrating pall under the low cloud. Except where the roof had collapsed and taken some masonry with it, almost all the four stone walls of the house remained standing. Blackened, windowless and doorless. The all-timber combined barn and stable, and the building in which Donald Kemp made and stored his corn liquor and cider, had been reduced to elongated heaps of charred ash. The corral and flanking apple orchards out back were still being layered with the fine black and grey detritus that had been carried up on the hot air. To where some faint breeze had drifted the ash in that direction.

Very little of the much-diminished heat of the flames reached across the yard to the start of the track where the three men stood for a few more moments: watching as the enclosed wagon came to a brief halt alongside the flatbed that had been abandoned by Kemp and England. The pause was for no longer than three seconds, before the sight of the three coffins acted to urge Bishop to demand an abrupt and swift re-start by the pair of fine greys.

'Sonofabitch, my folks,' the uniformed man groaned.

'I'll go bring them down, Corporal,' Edge told him. 'If you want to start doing what you have to here?'

'Appreciate it.'

'Guess I'd better have a look around for evidence,' England muttered pessimistically. And got rid of the ugly mess of chewed-out tobacco. 'Even if there's not a chance in a million of finding any.'

The half-breed went up across the fields, back-tracking at a far easier pace than he had come down into the hollow. He first retrieved his own gelding and elected to lead rather than ride him up to the trail. He hitched him to the rear of the flatbed become a hearse, and then drove the wagon to where the track cut off the trail. He left it there to go on foot toward the grassy area where the three once fire-spooked horses were now cropping contentedly. The saddle-broke piebald gelding that had been the last to

86

escape the blazing barn was the most skittishly nervous of Edge's approach. But he followed along in the wake of the two big brown and white Clydesdale stallions as Edge led them with a hand fisted to each stout bridle. Then the highly-strung animal submitted to being hitched alongside the others at the rear of the wagon. Edge had to cut some lengths of rope from his lariat to achieve this.

By the time he was back up on the seat and ready to start down the track, there was just an occasional flicker of flame to be seen among the blackened debris of the burnt-out buildings. But the closer he drove to the scene of destruction, the stronger was the acrid taint of smoke in the chill air of the murky afternoon. The horses that had experienced the terrors of the fire at its height communicated their apprehension to those that had come late and been allowed to remain at a distance.

Edge halted the wagon close to a hundred yards short of where the track entered the yard. And remained on the seat, smoking his cigarette down to a butt which he arced away as the scowling Larry England trudged toward him.

'It's like I said, Edge,' the Pomona lawman growled. 'Not a thing left to show anything about who lynched the Kemp family. And then came back here and set light to the place.'

'Guess the fire is proof enough that the guilty parties are Pomona people,' the half-breed said.

'Far as I'm concerned, there never was very much doubt about that,' England answered. And now toyed with the scar on the side of his jaw instead of the more usual moustache as he peered pointedly up at Edge. 'The killers wouldn't have taken the risk and trouble to come out here and start the fire if they'd never known I was about to start an investigation. And I'm not blowing my own trumpet, Edge!'

There was latent anger in his dark eyes: but no sign that he wanted to be given a reason to explode it here and now.

Edge shrugged and said evenly: 'No sweat, Sheriff.'

'Almost from the first day I drifted into Pomona, I found out about the bad feeling there was between the townspeople and the Kemp family. Stemmed from how the Kemps were religious pacifists and never gave a hand when there was the Indian troubles. You know about that?'

'For a share of my whiskey in the Black Hat, I was being told.'

'Willy Casey?'

'Right.'

'Then you probably heard it all just the way it was. If Willy wasn't fallen down drunk yet. He was here at the start of it and he was crippled by the –'

'Yeah, he told me,' Edge cut in as Harry Kemp appeared at a rear corner of the roofless shell of the house, and paused to glance toward the wagon before he moved into the orchard east of the corral.

'Lot of hypocrisy in any small town,' the sheriff went on. 'Pomona's not exceptional in that way.'

'Were you a lawman in many of them?'

England had started to look away from Edge, toward the uniformed man who was moving among the leafless fruit trees, with a short-handled shovel carried at his side. Suddenly he snapped his head around to stare at the half-breed, suspicion of an implied criticism seen against the latent anger in his dark eyes. But then he accepted an almost imperceptible arching of his eyebrows by the man on the wagon seat as a sign that there was no ulterior motive behind the query.

'I was never a lawman anyplace until I walked into the job at Pomona. Started out to study law – way, way back. But hitting books just didn't hold any appeal for me. Taught in a couple of grade schools in Philadelphia. Worked on the New Orleans docks. Then the Mississippi riverboats for a year or so. Some cowpunching over in east Texas. Next hired out on some farms. Some like this one, but never so tightly run. On my way across the state.'

88

Now he had gazed off to the side. And from the tone of his voice it was scenes from his past he was seeing rather than Harry Kemp as the cavalry corporal worked rhythmically at digging a trench in the orchard. Then England abruptly realised his mind was wandering away from the subject and he broke off. And there was sheepishness in his expression as he glanced surreptitiously at Edge before he hurried on:

'Anyway, I never claimed to the people of Pomona that I'd been anything that I wasn't. And I'm not saying now that whoever murdered the Kemps and burned the place is over worried about me being some kind of expert investigator. There's a whole bunch of citizens been nursing a grudge against the Kemps for a lot of years. Not to kill them, maybe. But they'd rather the Kemps weren't around. Run them out of the area. And that's what I mean about hypocrisy, Edge. The Kemps would have been sent packing years ago if it wasn't for the fine, fresh food they produced here. And didn't charge anything near top dollar for it. And the corn liquor and cider, too. Made a lot of people – women as well as men, I know – overlook they had cause to hate the Kemps.'

'Until last night,' Edge prompted. And swung down from the wagon. Blew into cupped hands and then began to beat his arms across his chest. 'When a bunch of them figured they couldn't allow –'

'A bunch of them?' England cut in. 'What makes you –'

'Okay, maybe just two,' the half-breed said as he moved to the side of the wagon. 'But more than one. Three people were strung up from that tree in the yard. Before the house was torched, there wasn't any sign of a struggle inside.' He nodded at the three pine caskets aligned on the rear of the wagon. 'And aside from them being dead of broken necks, there's nothing about the corpses that . . .' He dragged one of the coffins forward so that it jutted out over the side of the wagon.

89

'My God, I don't want to see for myself!' England blurted anxiously.

'Didn't plan to show you, feller. Was just about to say that it looks like these three people gave in to being hanged without kicking against what was happening. And it's my guess it likely took more than one lyncher to do the stringing up.'

The sheriff absently nodded his agreement with the contention.

'That a grave the corporal is digging out in the orchard?'

'What . . .? Oh. Yeah. Doesn't matter to him the place has been burned down. He said he was going to try to find a shovel and bury his family out here anyway.'

'Okay. The horses ain't over eager to go any closer to the fire stinks. You want to give me a hand to carry the boxes to the graveside?'

'Yeah, sure.'

He moved to get a grip on the other end of the coffin as Edge hauled it off the wagon. Then the two of them went at an awkward, short stepping, sidewise gait down to the end of the track and across the yard. Between the well and the front corner of the house. Out past the corral fence to where Kemp was working at a steady pace again after a brief pause to glance toward the men bringing the coffin. The uniformed man was breathing hard, but the cold of the afternoon immediately dried any sweat that might be oozing from his pores. His clothing, hands and face were blackened. But not by the rich soil he was scooping out of the hole he was digging. Instead, soot from when he had searched among the fire ashes for the shovel. A shovel with the handle shortened by being more than half burned away in the fire.

'Appreciate what you're doing to help,' Kemp said breathlessly.

'You're welcome,' Edge growled as England moved away after acknowledging the gratitude with a nod. And the half-breed remained beside the half-dug grave for perhaps two seconds more. Before he turned away with a less pronounced nod of his own – satisfied that one particular memory of Jamie was as dead and buried as was his corpse.

'You're right, of course,' England said as he started to move alongside Edge after waiting for him to catch up. 'The fire is solid proof that local people killed the Kemps. After the lynchings, they figured it could be several days – even weeks – before the crime was discovered. And when it was, there wouldn't be too much of an investigation carried out. Never was cause for me to investigate anything before and so I guess the people in town – all of them and not just the lynchers – never believed . . .'

They were back beside the wagon and the big man in the too-tight frockcoat seemed to have lost the thread of what he was saying. He peered out across the fields toward the trail at the lip of the hollow where it went out of sight toward Pomona, apparently having forgotten for the moment about the chore he had agreed to do.

'If it matters what I think,' Edge started.

'Uh?' England grunted, and was startled back to reality.

'There ain't a hell of a lot of point in worrying about what might have been,' the half-breed went on. He dragged a second coffin over the side of the wagon and the lawman came hurriedly forward to take the end before it crashed to the ground.

'Maybe the people that elected you were right, feller,' Edge continued in response to the quizzical look in England's gaze as they began to tote the coffin down the gentle incline of the track. 'Maybe you would have gone along with the general opinion in town: what most of the decent, law-abiding, small-minded hypocrites figured it suited themselves to believe.'

'Look, I –'

'That some passing through saddle-tramp did everyone a favour and strung up the Kemps,' Edge pressed on, his tone of voice even but strangely resolute in its lack of emotion. 'But the son of the family happened to come home. And I happened to be riding by. And you chose to come out here and investigate the killings.'

They were close to the graveside and the half-breed broke off and vented a soft sigh of relief as he stooped – and the pensively frowning England imitated the move – to lower the second coffin beside the first.

'It's going to take awhile,' Harry Kemp announced without turning away from his labours in the hole that was now some six feet square and as yet only eighteen inches down at its deepest corner.

'You want us to spell you?' Edge asked him.

'Like to do it myself, if I can. I'll let you know.'

'No sweat, Corporal.'

The two men left the third to the digging of the grave and walked slowly back toward, and then between, the charred remains of the farmhouse and its outbuildings. No flames showed anywhere now, and just an occasional wisp of grey smoke rose from among the debris. The smoke was a lighter shade of grey than the clouds. And of the day, too: for the afternoon was just beginning to give way to evening.

Back up at the wagon, Edge rested an elbow on the rim of a rear wheel and delved for the makings. England grunted and nodded, continued to frown: but was obviously concerned with the decision he had made rather than with the conflict of ideas that demanded he make a choice.

'You're right, mister,' he said with determination.

'That only really matters to me when it's my ass on the line, feller,' the half-breed answered.

'Which it has been, a whole lot of times,' England countered, and something close to a self-satisfied smile lit his dark eyes and altered the line of his mouth that was almost hidden by the thick moustache. 'Whereas mine hasn't.' He nodded emphatically. 'Yeah, I guess what I'm trying to get around to saying is that I'm really glad I'm not sitting back in my nice warm office now. With a

92

safe, easy job. Waiting for the call to come eat a fine Thanksgiving Supper at the meeting hall.'

He found what was left of the plug of tobacco he had been biting pieces off since starting out from town. And peered up the slope of the hollow with a look of grim determination now as he began to chew. Then turned his head to gaze levelly at the half-breed to qualify: 'Although I'm not saying that's how it would have been for me. Even if I'd found out about the killings some other way. Without Harry Kemp or you happening by the way you did.'

Edge struck a match on the wheelrim to light his cigarette. Replied on a stream of tobacco smoke: 'No sweat. I'm not claiming any credit for anything. Just aim to have it believed by local people that I didn't lynch Kemp and his wife and daughter. And I figure that'll be easier to do if the local sheriff finds out who the killers are.'

'I wouldn't be out here now if it wasn't my intention to see justice done,' England defended, ready to snarl an angry retort if this drew a response he didn't like.

'I'm not saying anything different, feller,' Edge countered. 'But intending to do something and getting down to doing it are two different things, seems to me.'

'No argument with that, Edge.'

'And a feller that doesn't have peace of mind about what he's doing can't apply the whole of his mind to what he's doing?'

'Yeah. Sure. That's right. But I have peace of mind about it now. Like you say, there's nothing to be gained by being concerned about what might have been. Maybe I won't be sleeping so comfortably for awhile now. But I'll be sleeping with a clear conscience.'

'Happy for you,' Edge growled sardonically.

'The hell with you, mister!' England rasped. And spat some tobacco juice at the side of the track. But there was no rancour in his voice. And in his dark eyes there was the suggestion of a knowing smile. 'You helped me to cut through all the side issues and get my thinking about this mess straightened out. So, all right . . . for your kind, helping people goes against the grain?'

'Let's get this third box down to Kemp,' Edge said evenly, flailing his arms across the front of his body.

'I've met quite a number of guys like you since I left teaching school and started drifting west.'

'Not many like me, feller,' the half-breed corrected. And now blew into his hands without taking the cigarette from between his lips. 'But everyone's entitled to their own opinions. I've told you a couple of mine, that's all. You want to make them yours, too, that's fine.'

'You aren't the kind to offer opinions without good reason, Edge,' England accused, the hint of a smile now gone from his face. And he fingered the old scar on his jaw.

'You're absolutely right, feller.'

'Nor to swap words just to kill some time?'

'Right again. But now you've got your head straightened out, maybe you can give some thought to killing time.'

'Uh?'

'I'm new around here. You've been around a little longer. Talked to more people than just Casey. The Indian trouble that set the town against the Kemps was somewhere near twenty years ago. The Kemps were lynched just last night or early this morning. Why after all those years of grudge carrying? Why did they decide that was the time for killing the Kemps?'

'Damnit, you're right again!' England exclaimed. 'I never gave that a thought!'

Once more he had to move quickly to grasp an end of a coffin before Edge dragged it far enough off the wagon side to drop it.

'That's because you were too busy thinking if you'd done right or wrong to come out here, feller,' the half-breed reminded. 'Now you're thinking straight. So I figure you ought to be able to give some thought to the reason you came?'

'Right again!' England said enthusiastically as the two of them moved away from the wagon.

'Nobody's perfect, so I'll tell you what, feller?'

'Yes?'

'Since we're toting a corpse in a coffin between us?'

'Yes?'

Edge's narrowed eyes glinted in the fading light of afternoon merging into evening. And this may have been part of a fleeting smile as he growled: 'What d'you say we make those the last rights?'

Eight

IT WAS full night when the cavalry corporal finished burying his parents and sister. But the threequarter moon was working harder to punch a hole in the clouds than the sun of the day had done. And in its pale light, Edge and Larry England were able to clearly see the wearily moving form of Harry Kemp as he completed the infill of displaced dirt – then used the back of the shovel to thus smooth the mound of the grave.

For no more than five seconds after the arduous chore of many hours was done and he had marked the burial place by pushing the shovel, handle-first, into the ground, the bereaved man stood with his campaign hat removed and his head bowed. Then he spun around and strode purposefully out of the orchard, across the yard between the burnt outbuildings and up the lower stretch of track to the wagon. Which was flanked by the half-breed and the lawman – Edge astride his own gelding and England sitting his own saddle cinched to the back of the Kemp family piebald.

The corporal's mount was free of the wagon traces and saddled with the army issue tack. The other team horse had also been taken from the traces and was hitched with the two Clydesdales to the rear of the wagon.

'Figured you wouldn't mind loaning me the mount, Kemp?' England asked of the grim-faced uniformed man.

The extent of Kemp's physical exhaustion was plain to see from the sluggish manner he climbed into his saddle. And he was too emotionally drained to alter the grim set of his broken-nosed, heavily-bristled and darkly-sooted face, or to speak in more than a dull monotone when he allowed: 'It's okay, Sheriff. You're welcome.'

'Any reason we shouldn't turn the other animals loose?'

'Sure. Let them roam. I've got no use for them right now.' He tugged on the reins to turn his horse away from the wagon, and the fire-charred scene of destruction and the three-casket grave. And his voice started to become husky with anguish when he added: 'I got no use for any lousy thing except finding out who murdered my family.'

He viciously spurred his horse into an immediate gallop up the track, and Edge and England followed with a lot less haste after the half-breed had unhitched the three animals from the rear of the wagon.

Kemp was not so distraught that he lost his bearings. He steered his horse into a right turn at the top of the track, to head east along the trail toward Pomona. And he regained some kind of composure again before he ran his mount into the ground. For he was waiting for Edge and England only about a half mile along the trail: his horse breathing hard from the gallop but not in any distress.

'Sorry about that,' he muttered sheepishly as he finished scrubbing at his sooted face with the yellow kerchief. And grimaced at his hands which were deeply ingrained with dirt.

'No sweat, Corporal.'

'Still making allowances, Kemp.'

The three of them moved along the trail at an easy walk, the expelled breath of men and horses showing as short-lived clouds of grey mist in the cold, clear moonlight. The clouds in the sky had gone south to pile up in a distant bank. The clop of hooves and the occasional creak of leather allowed for talk without need for voices to be raised. But there were few exchanges on the way to Pomona.

England said morosely: 'The fire destroyed any evidence the killers might have left, Kemp.'

'Has to be why it was set,' Kemp answered.

Edge said: 'The cider press was made of heavy lumber. It was burned up badly, but it was still recognisable for what it was.'

'So what?' Kemp queried wearily.

'*Still!*' England blurted, and snapped a finger and thumb. 'Your people made corn liquor as well, Kemp! Cider press would be too heavy to steal. But the still? That's something else.'

The uniformed man was confused for a few more moments. Then gave a sudden nod of understanding. 'It was made of metal. Even if it was right at the heart of the fire, there would have been some trace of it left?'

'That's exactly it,' the lawman replied, less forceful now. 'Doesn't prove anything until we find it, but it gives us something solid to work on.'

There followed several minutes of comfortable silence between the riders as each thought his own thoughts without emanating any hint of tension to disturb the others. Until Edge, continuing to keep an apparently casual watch over their surroundings, drawled:

'We figured out something else that could point up who killed your family, Corporal. Matter of why the lynchings took place when they did.'

'I don't get it,' Kemp complained.

'Why did it happen last night?' the lawman explained. 'Your parents stirred up bad feelings against themselves a lot of years ago. Why did –'

'Goddamnit, that surely is highly important!' the non-com cut in. 'If we can find that out, it could make a difference!'

There was no further talk for a longer period now. Nobody said anything, even when they rode past the horse

98

carcases at the scene of the ambush. And they were on the curve of the trail between the mesa-like rock formation and the rim of the plateau on which Pomona was sited before England ended the silence. Spoke as if after long and deep thought.

'I guess one strong possibility that has to be considered is that the lynchings had nothing to do with that old Indian trouble?'

'Yeah, Sheriff,' Kemp agreed without need to think about it. 'I figured it that way, too. How about you, pal?'

'Close enough,' Edge replied. 'Why not?'

Because of the hard, glittery brightness of the moon, the town lights did not radiate a visible aura. So if a total stranger to this part of west Texas came in on the trail from El Paso tonight, he would not realise Pomona was so close until he crested the rise and was able to see the cluster of buildings, the nearest of them about a half mile away.

It was to be expected that on such a frosty clear night, with the moon just a quarter short of full, that the sky above a small town would show little sign of the community below, with a dome of fringe glow. There was, this trio of riders saw as they neared the start of the western stretch of Main Street, the expected pall of dark smoke layered over the town. But the fires were burning only to combat the coldness of the night. For when they came closer still, none of them was able to detect any tantalising aromas of food being cooked on the stoves and ranges that gave off the smoke.

Then they were close enough to read the legend painted, red against blue and white, on a strip of canvas strung twenty feet above the ground between the two poles that marked the point where the open trail became the western end of Main Street. And Edge, for one, recalled another sign seen earlier in the day at the meeting hall: and remembered, too, something Larry England had said while reflecting on the almost certain loss of his star because of the

99

principles he felt went with the job. The sign read, in diminishing sizes of lettering:

POMONA THANKSGIVING SUPPER
At Town Meeting Hall
Tonight
Come one – Come all
Townspeople and Strangers all Welcome

'You know something?' Kemp asked rhetorically in an embittered tone as he kept his head tilted, reading the sign with scowling eyes until he and the two men flanking him had ridden beneath it.

'What?' England asked absently, his attention elsewhere as he surveyed the line of widely-spaced large houses on the right and the many more, crowded together ones that stretched along the other side of the street. Apprehensive about his job again, and searching out a first sign of whether the threat of losing it had been made a reality.

'It's almost like that banner up there is rubbing it in about my folks. Like the people here won't really be having the same kind of Thanksgiving as everyone else in the United States tonight.'

'Can see how you'd be likely to think that, Kemp,' England said, despondent after he had seen nothing to encourage him during his careful study of the street. 'But it's the same sign that was put up there last year. A little the worse for wear then, so I guess it was used a few years before that.'

'I can remember something like it,' Kemp admitted. 'From when I lived out at the farm.' He shook his head, as if trying to physically jerk himself free of the mood of self-pity that affected both him and England. 'I'm not saying it was especially done for this year. Just seems like it could have been, the way things are.'

The talk ended again, and the silence was disturbed only by the sounds of the horses' unhurried progress – louder

100

now as the clop of hooves, the creak of leather and an occasional soft whinny resounded off the façades of the flanking houses. Each man either imagined or was certain he sensed more than just a few pairs of eyes peering surreptitiously at them. Eyes that were hostile or nervous or sympathetic or impassive.

But none of the watchers was visible at any of the light-spilling undraped windows. And certainly nobody was seen on the street. Until the new arrivals reached the mid-town fork: where the narrower Old Pomona angled to the right and the commercial stretch of Main ran off at the other side of the stand of stunted pines.

The skinny form of Blanche Crabbe, stooped with age, could be seen silhouetted against the light of the open doorway of her small corner candy store. And the angry challenge that her arms-akimbo stance suggested was more forcefully emphasised in her strident tone of acrimony when she complained: 'I'm surprised at you, Lawrence England! Man that don't do what's told him by them that employ him don't deserve to keep his job! Only right and proper!'

A look of anguish came briefly to the black-eyed, thickly-moustached face of the former town sheriff. Then anger displaced it. But somebody else spoke before he was able to snarl a retort at the old woman.

'Hush now, dear lady. This is a matter of official business.'

This advice was offered by Father James O'Donnell as he emerged from a small house on the other side of Old Pomona. His time-ravaged, hollow-eyed face expressed anxiety. His shabby vestments were partially hidden by a ragged topcoat.

The attention of the three riders was held only briefly by the priest as he moved off toward his church. For a moment later all were drawn to peer toward the area out front of the law office: where the street was well illuminated by the moon, a little light spilling out of the office and a great deal more coming from the meeting hall next door. Just as earlier in the day, when Edge, England and Kemp left town, a group of men stood on the sidewalk before the law office. But just four of them were there tonight. And one of these had purposefully attracted the attention of the riders by hefting up a bundle of something from the sidewalk and tossing it down on to the street.

Edge said evenly as they angled to the left of the stand of timber: 'Guess when you get fired from office, it follows you're going to get evicted from it.'

'Everything that happens makes it more certain that my folks were murdered by Pomona –' Kemp started to snarl softly.

England cut in contemptuously: 'You can expect anything of a town that allows a travelling whorehouse to set up business in its public park.'

The garishly-coloured wagon in which Jim Bishop transported Brenda and Molly around the country was drawn up on an area of heavily trampled grass between the cannon on its plinth and the Protestant church. Its chequerboard-patterned rear door was toward the street and the steps were in position. The team of big greys were out of the traces, presumably lodged in the livery stable. The drapes were drawn across the window in the door and over those at the sides of the luridly painted vehicle, but yellow lamplight glimmered through an occasional chink. One such chink, in the door window, was momentarily darkened as the three men rode by: to signal they were being watched from the rig.

Apart from the meeting hall and the law office, the only other buildings on this stretch of Main Street that showed lamplight were The Black Hat Saloon and the Rio Grande boarding house down near the far end.

Just before the riders angled their mounts away from the centre of the street to head for the quartet of men out front of the law office, a movement down at the saloon captured their attention. But they were distracted for just a few moments, as they recognised the limping figure of Willy Casey after the man had pushed out through the batwings and stepped lop-sidedly down on to the street.

'In there are all your personal belongings we found in the office, England,' the short and fat, grey-eyed and sour-mouthed Ralph Lasky announced tautly, and gestured with a pudgy hand toward the string-tied, blanket-wrapped bundle on the street. 'You had fair warning. You've been removed from office by unanimous vote of the entire town council. It was agreed at the same time that you should be given a month's pay. Money's in with your property.'

The mayor of Pomona wore a different suit from that of the afternoon. It was a dark colour and looked more stylish and much more costly. There was no derby on his near bald head tonight. Backing him for the firing of Larry England was the just as flabby and only slightly taller Otis Boone. He, too, had changed his suit for tonight – funereal black again, but not so threadbare. The man named Jake, with the liver-spotted face, wore the same duster as in the afternoon. From the way in which it hung on his tall, skinny frame it didn't look like he was carrying a gun in either side pocket tonight. The fourth member of the group was the most anxious for the dismissal of England to be completed. He was the oldest, with silver hair and moustache, watery eyes that blinked a great deal and a pouting mouth that moved almost as much as his eyelids because of a nervous tic. His stockily-built body was encased against the cold by a dark-coloured, fur-collared coat buttoned from the throat to the hem that was just above his ankles.

'Wasn't no unanimous vote to pay you past today,' the scowling man with liver spots sneered.

'Figure he wouldn't expect the meanest man in Texas to vote to give him his proper dues, Jake Driscoll,' Kemp countered in a similar tone.

'Best you stay out of this, young man,' Lasky said

gravely. And directed a sidelong glance at Driscoll that warned him to be quiet, too.

'You getting rid of me for doing the job I was hired for?' England asked, and there was a quality of weariness in his voice now. Almost as if he were as eager as the silver-haired old-timer for the business to be over and done with quickly. But this was a point he felt he had to make.

Edge dug the makings from his shirt pocket and shifted his glinting-eyed gaze away from the four men grouped on the sidewalk. First peered in through one of the windows that flanked the open doorway of the meeting hall. And saw a section of a long table, covered with a white cloth and set with knives and forks. As he saw this, he became aware for the first time of a mouth-watering fragrance of cooking meat. And he allowed this smell to draw his gaze toward its source – the Rio Grande boarding house across the end of Main Street from the saloon.

'No, Larry,' Otis Boone began to reply to England. 'Dereliction of duty is the reason we felt –'

'My God, I was doing my duty by looking into a killing of –' England broke in.

This as Edge was about to return his attention to the exchange. But found himself drawn to do a double-take along the street. To where Willy Casey, lit only by the moon, was making awkward but inexorable progress between the pool of lamplight provided by the saloon and boarding house and that splashed out from the meeting hall. He was garbed in the same much mended coveralls as before, but now wore a ragged suit jacket that was just as ill-fitting on the upper half of his emaciated frame. His right hand was fisted around the top of the stout cane that enabled him to walk: unsteadily but without falling, despite his dead right leg. In his left hand was a twin barrel shotgun that he carried low at his side, parallel with the ground.

'You deserted this town to deal with an affair that Pomona people decided was none of their business,' the mayor interrupted in an officiously grave tone. 'If nothing untoward had happened while you were gone, it's possible we may have delayed the council meeting. Even called a committee of enquiry first. Where you could've put your case for acting against the wishes of the town.'

'But I –' England attempted to interject.

'You'll allow me to have my say!' Lasky commanded, his heavily fleshed face flushing with the temper he had come close to losing. This after Harry Kemp and Otis Boone and the silver-haired old-timer had been drawn to peer at Casey as the lame-legged man limped into the light from the meeting hall. 'I have to tell you that while you were gone, a peripatetic whoremaster came to town, mister! Brought his two disease-ridden, Godless, immoral women into Pomona with him! Felt free to set up his house of ill-repute on wheels in the very park where our decent women, the mothers of our children, are insulted by the sight of what . . .'

Lasky's righteous rage was bubbling up close to the surface and his voice was rising toward the volume and tone of an indignant speech before he suddenly realised he had lost the attention of most of his audience. And he allowed his tirade to hang incomplete in the abruptly tense air – aware that his anger was not the reason for the atmosphere of unease that had infiltrated the chill night air.

'What it comes down to, England, is that you've been fired and we want your badge so we can give it to the new –' the duster-coated Driscoll started to snarl. Before he, too, felt the compulsion to break off and stare at Casey. But he failed to sense the tension that was generated by the determined progress of the shotgun-toting man. And he began to add: 'Well, speak of the devil and –'

Edge struck a match on the stock of his Winchester that jutted out of the forward hung boot. Lit the cigarette.

The silver-haired oldster, eyes blinking and tic twitching faster than ever, hissed: 'Do shut up, Jake!'

'You made Willy sheriff?' England rasped incredulously.

Edge called: 'How you doing, feller?'

'Fitting you should come and join us here, Sheriff Casey,' the mayor said, trying for a commonplace tone. But his voice was husky with nervousness.

The lame man had glanced just once toward the four men on the sidewalk and the three astride horses in front of them. And now, as he continued to limp along an unwaveringly straight course on the far side of the wide street, he kept peering directly ahead. Sounded a little breathless, but pronounced his words with the clarity of a well practised drunk when he replied: 'I ain't doin' so bad right now, stranger. Can't join you for a couple of minutes, Mr Lasky. Official business to attend to. Was invited to stand for sheriff, Mr England. Nobody else stood against me, so . . .' He seemed to lose the thread of what he was saying. Sighed, and completed: 'So . . . there you go.'

His back was toward the group across the street when he was through with the response. And he was beyond the cemetery and passing the front of the church.

'What do you think he means? Official business?' It was the silver-haired man who asked this, his voice low and tremulous.

'How the hell do we know, Brad?' Driscoll growled. 'Drunk as a skunk, looks like.'

'Where did he get that shotgun?' Boone muttered.

'Looks like Jo Sinclair's,' Lasky supplied.

'Sonofabitch, this whole thing gets crazier by the moment,' Kemp rasped. Then backed his horse out from between the other two and turned him. 'I need a drink.'

But he checked his move to spur the animal forward. And turned in the saddle to peer in the same direction as the rest of the men when Willy Casey shouted:

'Hey, you in the pretty coloured wagon! Have somethin' to tell you!'

He had come to a halt just beyond the fringe glow of the meeting hall light. But he could be seen clearly in the moon glow. Stood rigidly erect, fifteen feet back from the rear of the wagon: facing it. His right hand thrust his cane hard against the ground to keep his balance as he swung the shotgun up to cant it to his shoulder.

'Oh, my,' Boone gasped.

His words barely audible, the nervous Brad whispered: 'Ralph, there's going to be a tragedy if you don't do something.'

He punctuated his ominous prediction with a strangled cry as the door of the brightly-painted wagon swung open and a shaft of lamplight fell toward Casey. The voice of Molly was heard, indistinctly, for a moment. Before she silenced herself in mid-protest as Jim Bishop stooped out through the doorway and stood on the top tread of the steps. He was hatless now, and had removed the caped ulster and the jacket of his suit. He was otherwise fully dressed, even though the way he yawned and rubbed the inside corners of his eyes with a finger and thumb suggested he had been sleeping.

'Hell, what's all the shoutin' about, man?' he demanded irritably. Then did a double take at Casey.

'Jim,' Molly called softly, and the tone of warning was clearly heard despite the thickness of her voice from the head cold.

No longer shouting, and again enunciating his words with great care, the lame man replied to the dude: 'There's a law against whores in Pomona, mister. So it's my duty to ask you and your women to leave town.'

'Your duty?' Bishop exclaimed, and a grin spread across his ruggedly hewn face.

'Was elected sheriff today.'

'Sheriff? Hell, that's a laugh!' His grin broadened and at night the whiteness of his teeth showed up even more starkly against his element-darkened complexion.

'You wanna laugh, that's your right, mister,' Casey countered as the full-bodied blonde and the skinny brunette showed in the doorway behind the dude. 'I take my new job pretty seriously.' He noisily sucked in some night air. 'Askin' you polite. Hitch up your team and pull outta Pomona before folks start to gather for the Thanksgivin' supper.'

The grin was instantly displaced by a scowl. And Bishop jerked his head to peer at the group gathered out front of the law office. Demanded in scornful tones to know: 'Is this drunken cripple the local village idiot?'

Then he stared fixedly at Casey again. As the blonde Brenda caught her breath and the black-haired Molly thrust out a clawed hand to hook it over Bishop's shoulder. This in response to the sinister metallic sounds of the double hammers of the shotgun being thumbed back.

'A tragedy, I tell you,' Brad murmured.

'Ralph?' Boone entreated helplessly.

Lasky seemed to be dumbstruck by the explosive situation. His face as grey as his eyes.

'The man's doin' what he was elected to do,' Jake Driscoll hissed through teeth clenched in a satisfied grin. 'Upholdin' the law.'

'My God,' England breathed, as the man newly elected to his former job brought down the shotgun from his shoulder.

'Can't do nothin' about my dead leg, mister,' Casey said, his voice taut with the effort he needed to take to keep his anger in check. 'But intend that the drinks I just had down at the Black Hat were my last.'

'Hell, sure,' Bishop countered, and continued to stare with fear-filled eyes at the levelled shotgun as he shook his shoulder to dislodge Molly's hand. Then managed to fix a wan grin on his features as he started to add: 'I was outta line, sayin' what I did about your affliction. Why don't we –'

'Asked you polite,' Casey cut in. 'It was you started in with the name-callin'. Tellin' you now, you fancy threaded sonofabitch! Hitch up your team and drag your ass outta this town! Along with them two clapped out whores!'

'Shit, Jim!' Brenda snarled. 'You don't have to stand

for that! That gun ain't even loaded, I bet! Folks wouldn't allow a drunken old crippled creep like him to –'

She thrust a long barrel revolver out of the doorway, between the frame and Bishop's upper arm. The glint of light on the highly polished metal of the gun distracted the attention of the dude. And the frown of fear that had replaced the insecure grin when the blonde began her enraged diatribe was transformed in part of a second into a mask of sheer terror.

In the same sliver of time, Willy Casey squeezed both triggers of the shotgun. Was sent into a backward sprawl by the recoil as the weapon exploded its double load toward the man on the steps. And as the lame man crashed hard to the winter ground, still clutching the damaging gun and the cane that had failed to keep him on his feet, Jim Bishop breathed his last. Did so as he was hurled backwards through the doorway by the flesh-tearing impact of the lead shot blasting into his belly. If he uttered any sound it was masked by the roar of the shotgun's double report and the screams of the two women who were sent staggering into the wagon by the forceful falling weight of the dead man.

Then came stretched seconds of total silence. While Casey remained unmoving and the men across the street gazed fixedly at the rear of the wagon from which the shaft of light spilled, again unimpaired, toward the new sheriff of Pomona. Because the body of the wagon was painted crimson, it was only on the white inside of the open door and on the unpainted steps beneath that the dead man's blood was clearly visible at a distance. And not just liquid blood. There were some blood-saturated pieces of tissue clinging to the woodwork, too. Also, some grey and white and yellow-hued fragments of what, moments ago, had been Jim Bishop's mid-section.

'God Almighty!' Larry England forced out through a shock-constricted throat.

'I told you so!' Brad hissed, his voice low but the words

bursting explosively from between his twitching lips. And there was a strange, childishly boastful quality about the silver-haired old man as he emphasised: 'Didn't I say so?'

'He's dead, you bastard!' Molly shrieked to confirm what everyone who had seen the massive wound blasted into the belly of the dude already knew. 'You killed him!'

'He got what he had comin' to him,' Jake Driscoll growled. But he had to swallow hard: perhaps to keep from getting sick to his stomach while he continued to stare fixedly at the blood and pieces of pulpy flesh spread over the door and the steps.

'Sonofabitch,' Kemp muttered.

Casey had struggled up into a sitting attitude. Now allowed the shotgun to remain on the ground while he used both hands on the cane to lever himself unsteadily upright. And defended in a high-pitched voice of anguish: 'They pulled a gun on me! I had to shoot! You all saw the gun!'

The revolver he was talking about now lay on the ground beside the foot of the crimson splashed steps. A nickel-plated Colt with a nine-inch barrel and ivory butt plates. Dropped from the hand of the shocked Brenda as she was toppled backwards by the dead weight of Bishop.

A crowd of curious people was gathering beside the stand of trees in the fork of the street. Men, women and some children. Hurrying there from Old Pomona and the western stretch of Main. They generated a hum of talk, the tenor of which was impossible to discern.

'This is awful, truly awful,' Boone said, shaking his head, his treble chins trembling.

'I'm with Jake,' Lasky announced and there was something approaching the former officiousness in his voice. 'The sheriff had no other choice but to shoot.'

He wrenched his gaze away from the blood-spattered rear of the wagon and began to search among the men close to him for more support for this view. But then he caught his breath, shocked again. This when he saw the

110

taciturn half-breed snatch the Winchester from the boot.

Kemp snarled: 'What the hell, pal?'

There was already a live round in the breech of the rifle. So Edge needed only to thumb back the hammer as he slammed the base of the stock into his shoulder. Then pressed his bristled cheek to the side of the stock. Aligned his eye behind the sights: squeezed the trigger.

The bullet hit the fallen Colt. Smashed into the angle where the trigger guard met the underside of the long barrel. And the impact sent the revolver skittering for five or six feet beneath the wagon. The shot had hit its target while the full-bodied Brenda was still dropping into a crouch after lunging out of the bloodied doorway and leaping down the steps – the hooked fingers of her reaching hand some six inches short of grasping the big Colt.

Edge pumped the lever action of the Winchester and the expended shellcase pinged to the sidewalk. And Brad leapt instinctively backwards, like he was terrified of the harmless tube of metal. The blonde continued down on to her haunches. Snapped her head around to stare with blazing eyes at the group of men across the street. Where the one who had denied her revenge still sat his horse and kept the muzzle-smoking rifle at his shoulder. There was another stretched second of utter silence. Before Brenda gaped her mouth wide and began to shriek:

'You friggin' –'

Molly recommenced to weep softly. And then Brenda rocked back off her haunches and on to her rump, her back against the side of the steps, her hands covering her fleshy face and her flabby body shaking with sobs.

'God Almighty,' England said again, staring at Edge now, as the half-breed slid the rifle back in the boot and drew hard against his almost burnt out cigarette.

There was a higher volume of talk among the crowd at the fork of the street. Once again the varying emotions of conflicting opinions cancelled each other out and the sound reached the men out front of the law office as just a neutral hubbub.

Willy Casey kept switching his gaze between the expanding bunch of townspeople, the multi-coloured wagon and the men. He looked at every moment on the brink of saying something, but seemed not to trust himself to speak.

'A tragedy,' Brad wailed softly. 'I knew it from the very start. I said it.'

'You made your point, Harrison,' Driscoll complained, voicing the impatience most were feeling toward the agitated man. 'You can see into the friggin' future.'

England had slowly unfastened the strained buttons of his frock coat. Now he unpinned the badge from his vest front and flipped it through a short arc so that it hit the front wall of the law office and bounced down to come to rest on the sidewalk between the glowering Driscoll and the grim-faced Lasky. The former sheriff of Pomona expressed something close to sympathy as he said:

'Seems to be the night for people to get what they ask for. Bishop got his. You wanted my badge, so . . .'

He allowed his voice to trail away. And then his moustached, dark-eyed face expressed contempt for the men on the sidewalk before he looked away from them so he could direct a forceful spit at the street.

'Wasn't no reason for a man to be shot dead,' Brad Harrison complained as England dismounted to claim his bundle of belongings.

Edge rasped the back of a hand over his bristled jaw and raked his glinting eyes over the faces of the quartet of men standing on the sidewalk. And the silver-haired old-timer took yet another step backwards, like he expected something more palpable than softly drawled words to come toward him. But that was all there was, as the half-breed murmured:

'Always is, feller. After a firing squad's done its work.'

112

Nine

IN THE wake of the killing of Jim Bishop most people continued to do whatever it was that had occupied them before the return to town of Edge, England and Kemp had first ruffled the surface of the calm evening of this Thanksgiving Day. But it was an uneasy peace that came to the town, bringing with it a sense of tension that had an almost palpable presence in the bitingly cold air that was not stirred by the slightest breeze on the open street.

Inside the Black Hat Saloon, within the area of comfortable warmth radiated by the lit stove, the half-breed, the deposed sheriff and the cavalry non-com had by tacit mutual consent instituted a separate enclave of serenity after the storm. Each of them content for talk to be barred from their small group after the anxious Joe Sinclair had been persuaded to break one of the house rules for the second time that day: and now was in the kitchen cooking up enough bacon and beans for three men.

The jittery bartender, who was sure he would not be able to face food for a long time after his shotgun was used to kill a man, was obviously affected by the tension that was tautly stranded through Pomona from one end to the other. And he created only low sounds as he worked carefully in the kitchen: like he was afraid that even too loud a rattle of a knife against a plate would trigger dire consequences. Louder sounds came occasionally from within the stove at which his trio of customers warmed themselves, as they sipped rye whiskey and thought their own thoughts.

From outside, mostly muffled by distance, came infrequent sounds that could be identified against the muted hum of a small town in the centre of a vast tract of silent country. Of raised voices, of doors opened and closed, of hooves against hard-packed dirt, or equine snorts, of timbers creaking, harness brasses jingling and wheels turning.

Then, as the youthful-looking Sinclair emerged from the doorway beneath the stairs – a tray laden with three plates held in front of him – the brightly-coloured wagon rolled past the saloon. Both whores rode on the outside seat, the blonde Brenda having charge of the two big greys in the traces. The skinny Molly a handkerchief to her face, blowing her nose. Probably because of her head cold rather than out of grief now. Neither woman glanced toward the saloon, although they would have seen the three saddled horses hitched to the rail out front.

Of the three men who looked out over the tops of the batwings, only Edge continued to keep his hooded eyes fixed in the same direction after the whorehouse on wheels had gone by. His implacable attention held by the sight of Cloris Snelling in her mourning garb as the short, stout woman moved with an almost regal manner out of the Rio Grande boarding house and started down the steps.

'Won't be such good grub as the women are cookin' up over at the boardin' house,' Sinclair announced as he set the tray down on the table before the stove. 'But then I don't provide food as a general rule. Like I said.'

'Good of you to do this for us, Joe,' England assured.

'That's right, pal,' Kemp added. 'Guess we wouldn't be welcome to the supper the way the sign claims. And I'm in no mood for any kind of thanksgiving, anyway.'

Each of the seated men took a plate of food off the tray and dragged his chair closer to the table.

'Enjoy,' Sinclair urged in the kind of tone and with the

114

kind of expression that indicated he did not think he would ever enjoy anything again.

Edge started right in to eat the heap of beans that had a few chunks of bacon in it. The food was hot and the coldness of the afternoon and evening since he had last eaten at this very table had given him an appetite for just such a meal. Like before, he was in no mood to appreciate subtle flavours. Neither were his fellow diners, but both were affected by the events of the day, and it took them a few moments of half-hearted eating before the hunger for food overcame the states of their minds. And they began to wolf it down with as much relish as the half-breed.

From behind the bar counter, Sinclair watched them with something akin to envy in his remarkably clear eyes, while his hands toyed nervously with the ends of his boot-lace tie. Then, after the meal was over and Edge washed down a final mouthful of bacon and beans with a swallow of whiskey and poured himself another, the bartender was startled into voicing a gasp of surprise. This when the batwings swung open and everyone looked toward the once bulky but now skinny figure of Willy Casey as the doors creaked closed on their dry hinges behind him. Only the previously withdrawn Sinclair was startled at the sight of the newly elected sheriff of Pomona. The other three occupants of the Black Hat had heard the thud of the man's cane and the drag of the foot of his lame leg as he mounted the steps and crossed the boardwalk.

Casey looked much as when they last saw him, except that the badge discarded by England was now pinned to the lapel of the ragged suit jacket he wore over his coveralls. And around his narrow hips there was a gunbelt, with a holster hanging down below the hem of the jacket on the right side. The barrel stuck out through a hole in the toe of the holster, and the distinctive ivory butt plates of the Colt that had caused a killing without being fired showed at the top. The butt jutted forward, so that Casey could draw it with his left hand while his right hand was fisted to the cane. But in his bony left hand at the moment was the frame of the double barrel shotgun: the weapon broken open to reveal that the twin breeches were empty, even of the expended shell cases.

On the loose-skinned face of the man was something of the same look of shock that had held him dumbstruck earlier. But in his grey eyes, amid their bloodshot surrounds, there was now a determination to get said what he needed to say this time. He directed just a sidelong glance toward the men at the table as England finished refilling his own glass with rye, then started to pour a fresh drink for Kemp at a nod from the cavalry corporal. Then Casey moved in his awkward but resolute gait to the bar counter. Where he set down the shotgun on the top and breathed a weary sigh before he told its owner:

'I appreciate the loan of the gun, Mr Sinclair. Way it turned out, you were right. Never should have taken it off you the way I did.'

'Whatever you say, Willy,' the bartender allowed, took the shotgun, snapped it closed and put it out of sight beneath the counter. 'You want a drink?'

'Does a hungry new-born baby want its mother's tit?' Casey said wistfully. But held up his free hand in a checking gesture when Sinclair turned to reach for a bottle. 'Thanks, but no thanks, Joe,' he went on hurriedly and there was more obvious regret in his voice at the need to refuse. He leaned his cane against the front of the counter. 'Oh, by the by, you'll get paid for the cartridges. Soon as the town gets back to normal after the holiday.'

His confidence seemed to increase with each word he spoke. And by the time he turned around, supporting himself with one elbow pushed backwards on the bartop, almost all sign of the shock at killing a man was gone from his slack face. 'Same as Otis Boone'll get paid out of town money for the buryin' of that Bishop guy.' Then he abruptly changed the subject to claim: 'It's stupid I should be wearin' this badge, Mr England.'

116

'That's what I thought when I first got elected to wear it, Willy,' England said evenly, and took out a chew of tobacco from the supply he had transferred from the bundle to a pocket of the frockcoat. 'You'll get used to the idea and maybe as time goes by you'll –'

'That was different,' Casey cut in. 'This was done out of spite. Got to admit, I went along with it on account of the money the job pays. Spite on their part against you. Joke on my part against them, I reckon. But it ain't nothin' like any kinda joke now. Not since I took it into my head to treat the job seriously. Just planned to run that Bishop and his whores outta town, that's all. But when I seen this here gun pointed at me . . .'

He patted the holster and shook his head as he allowed the sentence to hang unfinished in the stove-heated air of the once fine and now faded saloon. There had been ruefulness in his tone, but his feelings were far removed from maudlin self-pity. Now, as he looked directly at Edge who was rolling a cigarette, Casey's manner became suddenly impassive. 'Have to thank you for that real fine piece of shootin', mister. That whore would've shot me, sure as hell, if she'd gotten a hand to this here gun.'

'No sweat, feller.'

'I sure came out in a cold sweat myself, mister. When I seen her go for the gun and knew I'd used up both barrels on that Bishop guy.'

'First time you killed somebody?' Edge asked, and ran the tip of his tongue along the gummed strip of the cigarette paper.

'Not countin' Injuns. In a runnin' fight in the old days.'

Harry Kemp grimaced at the mention of the Indian troubles of the past.

'Figure you'll learn as you go along, feller.'

'If I don't get myself killed first.'

Edge struck a match on the top of the stove to light his cigarette. And replied on a stream of tobacco smoke: 'Always a chance of that.'

117

'Been a tough first day in what was always a pretty easy job, Willy,' England excused.

'Nearly was my first and last, Mr England. Still could be.'

'How's that, Willy?' Sinclair asked into a sudden tense atmosphere that Casey's flatly-spoken comment had created.

'Was sent here to arrest you, Mr Edge,' the new lawman said and his usually sad-looking, slack-fleshed face had probably never expressed a deeper degree of melancholy.

'Oh, my God,' England groaned.

Kemp rasped: 'Sonofabitch.'

Sinclair obviously wanted to move hurriedly out of the area immediately behind Casey. But seemed to be rooted to the spot. And all he could do was lean a little to the side.

The crippled man revealed something of the kind of tension that had been held in tight control beneath the veneer of great sadness. He breathed a just audible sigh of relief before he went on: 'To hold you on suspicion of murder. Don't guess you'd come quietly, uh?'

'Mostly I'm the quiet type, Willy,' Edge said evenly. 'In fact, almost the only times I get loud is when somebody makes me do something I don't want to.'

Casey sighed without any attempt to mask it now. And nodded as he glanced at Kemp and England and then over his shoulder at the bartender. 'I tried. Everyone here is a witness to that. Already been the one killin' in Pomona tonight. If I'd tried any harder to arrest Mr Edge, good chance of there bein' a second one.'

'And a second election of a new sheriff to boot, Willy,' Sinclair growled.

'Didn't I say that?' Casey snapped, and directed a censuring look over his shoulder at the abruptly cowed bartender. 'You figure I figure I could take this guy in a fair gunfight? I could only be that stupid if I was drunk out of

118

my skull. And since I blasted that guy to eternity I ain't never been so stone cold sober in my life.'

'So why go through the frigging motions?' Kemp demanded caustically.

'Like I told you, soldier,' Casey countered earnestly. 'Plan to take this job as sheriff seriously. Town council is payin' me and so I gotta try to do their biddin'. And when I was told to come down here to the saloon and arrest Mr Edge for killin' your folks, I had to –'

'Council being Ralph Lasky and Jake Driscoll in this case,' Sinclair put in dully. 'I'm on the council and nobody asked me what I thought about the lynchings.'

Casey nodded. 'Has to be said. While Lasky and Driscoll was in a huddle that ended with them tellin' me to come bring in Mr Edge, Otis Boone was busy takin' care of the remains of the whoremaster. And Harrison had to run to answer a call of nature.'

'He'll still be full of shit,' Sinclair growled and drew himself a beer.

'Seemed to me like the whole bunch of them are,' Kemp said.

'Don't let that opinion get loose in Pomona, Corporal,' Sinclair advised. 'Unless you count Ralph Lasky out of it.'

'Right,' England agreed. 'A whole bunch of people in town reckon that if he wanted to, Lasky could walk on water.'

'And there's some,' Casey added morosely, 'who figure he could whistle *Dixie* while he was walking on the water.'

There was a pause in the talk and until Joe Sinclair started out from behind the bar counter to collect the dirty dishes, the crackle and hissing of burning in the stove were the only sounds made within the Black Hat. While from outside the saloon came the hum of the town interspersed with an occasional burst of louder noise, muted by distance, of renewed preparations for the supper in the meeting hall. Just once during the half minute or so while the men in the saloon thought their private thoughts, some of them were drawn by the sound of footfalls to glance out over the tops of the batwings. And they saw a woman emerge from the Rio Grande boarding house. She was carrying two cloth-draped baskets that looked to be heavily laden. She went in the direction of the meeting hall. Those who did not immediately look away were able to see another woman as she appeared in silhouette at an upper story window of the boarding house. From her height and build she could have been Cloris Snelling, with the hat and veil gone from her head.

'You men were a long time out to the Kemp place,' Willy Casey asked abruptly. And seemed disconcerted when the men at the table all turned to look at him. Then he blurted: 'Damnit, it feels real strange me askin' these kinda questions. Specially of you, Mr England. But I got good reason.'

'Couldn't use the time looking for evidence, Willy,' England replied. And spat tobacco juice into the grate. Fingered the scar on his chin as he listened to the short-lived hissing sound of the dark-stained saliva vaporised by heat. 'Place was burning when we got there. We couldn't get near it until it was all burnt out.'

Sinclair began to gather up the dishes from the table.

'Hell, if he wants to play at being sheriff, let him go out there and do his own poking around, pal!' Kemp growled angrily. 'We've had our grub. It's about time we went to work on what we know. Instead of sitting here chewing the fat about stuff of no consequence.'

'That *we* doesn't include me anymore, Corporal,' England countered evenly and gestured toward the lame man at the bar. This as the bartender completed his chore at the table and carried the plates toward the doorway beneath the stairs. 'Willy's been given the job of Pomona's lawman in the same way I got it a year and a half ago. Back then, nobody had less faith in me being able to do the job as I did in myself. Willy wants to have a fair crack

120

of the whip and I reckon he should have the chance.'

England's dark eyes shifted from the scowling face of Kemp to the impassive features of Edge as he finished speaking. And the half-breed answered the tacitly implied question:

'So long as I can ride away from this neck of the woods without anyone figuring I just might have strung up the Corporal's folks, I don't care who has a hand in proving the point.'

Kemp rose angrily to his feet and strode to the batwings. But he did not push between them. Just hooked his hands tightly over their tops and peered fixedly into the moonlit street. In the kitchen, Joe Sinclair created small sounds as he washed the dishes. The sounds that came out of the meeting hall were less obtrusive within the Black Hat. The aroma of roast turkey that drifted across the street from the boarding house was a lot less appetising now the men had eaten.

'Honest, Mr England,' Casey urged. 'I got a real good reason for wantin' to know what happened out at the Kemp place.'

Edge had been about to pour himself another drink, but stayed the move. And both England at the table and Kemp at the doorway matched the intensity with which he gazed at Casey: all of them aware of the depth of feeling that gripped the man who had been nothing but the town drunk for so long.

'Who left town, Willy?' the half-breed asked evenly.

'We got bushwhacked on the way out there,' England said. 'A couple of sharpshooters killed two of our horses. Slowed us up some. Gave them time to set the fires in the house and barns.'

'To burn any signs of who lynched my folks,' Harry Kemp added. And was even more earnestly interested in Casey's attitude as the skinny man in the loose fitting coveralls and ragged, too-big jacket began to nod knowingly.

121

England said: 'But they didn't manage to cover it up that the corn liquor still was missing.'

'Who left town?' Edge asked again, more insistently.

'Left pretty soon after you three headed out with the bodies on the wagon,' Casey supplied. 'And ain't back yet, far as I know. Do know where they're likely to be, though. Them two Comanches that live down on Old Pomona.'

'Sonofabitch!' Kemp rasped.

'White Eagle and Black Hawk?' England growled. And nodded. 'They sure wouldn't pass up the chance of getting their hands on a liquor still, no doubt about that.'

'Where, pal?' Kemp demanded, cold menace in his eyes as he started to run the top of his thumb along the tips of his fingers close to the fastened flap of his holster. The tone of his voice caused both Edge and England to look at him. And they found him staring fixedly at Casey as he reminded: 'You said – if they aren't back in town, you know where they're likely to be?'

'Don't tell him,' England warned.

'Don't plan to,' Casey replied. 'Not so long as he's mad as he is right now.'

And although he was awkwardly slow, he was faster to get the long barrel Colt out of his holster than was Kemp to fumble for his revolver. For the younger man had managed only to unfasten the holster flap and get a hand on the butt of his gun before the newly-acquired weapon of the new sheriff was levelled at him. Then, for part of a second, it looked as if the uniformed man was going to carry through his draw to the end. But something about the degree of gravity on the loose-skinned face of Willy Casey – and the rock steadiness of his left hand fisted around the ivory-plated butt of the revolver – warned Kemp that the older man would kill him if he tried. And he dropped his hand slowly until it was hanging limply at arm's length down at his side.

'You over your anger now, soldier?' Casey asked evenly.

Kemp allowed a sigh to whistle out between pursed lips, and with it the tension was seen to drain from his body. He nodded.

'Old meeting ground of the Injuns when Texas all belonged to them. But you men should know I plan to be alongside whoever elects to go out there.'

'Twin Bluffs,' Kemp said.

'You got it,' Casey confirmed. And reached across the front of his flat belly to push the big Colt back into the holster. 'Glad you didn't figure I was trying the single kind just now.'

Kemp expressed a wan smile that did not touch his eyes as he replied: 'Only a fool would figure a bluff when he can see the other man's holding the winning card.'

Casey nodded. 'But sometimes a man gets so mad he can't see a thing he don't want to, soldier. And for awhile there all you saw, seemed to me, was that pair of Injuns.'

'Who maybe had nothing to do with killing your family, Corporal,' England said.

The fires of rage flared up again in the dark blue eyes of Harry Kemp. But before he could voice his scorn for the other man's opinion, Edge added:

'Could be the Indians didn't know about the lynchings until we hauled the bodies into town, feller. Could be it was only then they figured they had a chance to loot the place.'

'And burn it so nobody could figure if anythin' had been took,' Casey completed. 'The still and as many bottles of corn liquor as they could carry, if I know them Injuns.'

'And if they did have a hand in the fire out at the farm,' England added.

The new sheriff and the previous wearer of the five-pointed silver star exchanged knowing glances. And both Kemp at the batwings and Edge at the table saw this and were able to read clearly what was in the minds of Casey and England.

The cavalry non-com said coldly: 'Shit, far as you men are concerned, there's not a snowball's chance in hell of those two Comanches not having a hand in it!'

And he swung around on his heels and pushed out through the creaking doors.

'The soldier ain't wrong,' Casey growled, grasping his cane and starting away from the bar counter. And showed that he could move almost as fast as an able-bodied man over a short distance. He came to an abrupt halt at the doors that had ceased to flap in the wake of Kemp. Gazed outside in the direction of the hitching rail, and then looked back over his shoulder toward the table in front of the stove. Announced with unconcealed relief: 'It's okay. He's mounted up, but waitin'. You men comin' along?'

Edge dropped his cigarette butt in his empty shot glass and rose from the table. Called toward the doorway beneath the staircase at the far side of the saloon: 'Square up with you later, Sinclair!'

There had been silence from the Black Hat's kitchen since the man out there had finished the dishes. The same silence held in the wake of the half-breed's promise. Casey went out of the saloon and Edge moved toward the creaking doors. England held back to take another drink at a single swallow before he left the table. Said as he stepped out on to the porch:

'Reckon I'd feel bad about it if I didn't see it through.'

'Good to have you along, pal,' Kemp answered from where he sat his horse. 'You, too,' he added with a glance at Edge who was about to mount into his saddle. Then he looked toward Willy Casey, who was hobbling fast across the street toward the livery stable. 'I don't doubt he means well, but . . .' He shrugged and let the frown on his broken-nosed face fill out the rest of his opinion of the crippled man.

'The road to hell is paved with good intentions,' England quoted ruefully as he watched the awkwardly limping man. Then swung up astride his horse.

Edge blew into his cupped hands. Said as he turned up the collar of his coat: 'On a night cold as this, hell almost sounds good.'

This exhausted their fund of small talk while they waited for Casey to return with a mount. And afterwards they either peered into the middle distance or scanned the street which, when Casey had gone into the livery, was deserted. Until Joe Sinclair appeared on it from out of the town park beyond the church, saw the trio of mounted men and broke into a loping run. When he came to a breathless halt, Edge gave him a little time to recover from the exertion by saying:

'Pay for the grub and liquor when I get back, feller.'

The bartender nodded and waved a hand in a gesture to dismiss the subject. England and Kemp peered down at the man standing on the street, anxious to hear the news he was obviously eager to give.

'They didn't come back sure enough,' he blurted as, across and down the street, Willy Casey led a saddled horse out of the livery and began to get clumsily astride the animal. 'I went to the place they live and I asked a few people. Nobody's seen those two Comanches since soon after noon.'

Because it was so quiet on the street, the preparations for the Thanksgiving supper in the meeting hall apparently complete, Sinclair's voice carried a long way. The new town sheriff heard him and the commotion also brought the short, plump woman in black to the window of an upper-story room in the Rio Grande boarding house.

'White Eagle and Black Hawk didn't come back to Pomona,' England told Casey as the lame man rode up alongside the other mounted men.

'I heard what Joe said,' Casey acknowledged with tight-lipped satisfaction. 'So I called it right, uh? Them two birds have flown again.'

Edge's mind was suddenly host to a vivid memory of how it had played tricks on him during his drinking jag in the barn last night, as he drawled: 'And if they stole some of Donald Kemp's ready-made corn liquor, by now they could be flying pretty damn high.'

Ten

THE MEETING ground of the old-time Indian nations that once ranged free over Texas before the Spanish crossed the Rio Grande to colonise the country was to the south of the town.

At first out along the trail that started where the street known as Old Pomona ended. The four horsemen remained on this trail for a few minutes, until it swung away to the east. Then they angled off it to ride over an expanse of dead-looking terrain. Of rocks and rock-hard earth with hardly a sign of vegetation to be seen. Once off the trail there was no clear way among the ridges and ravines, outcrops and hollows that comprised the ruggedly crumbled southern slope of the plateau on which Pomona was sited – to a stranger in the area like Edge, anyway. But Casey and Kemp, who rode side by side ahead of the half-breed and England, followed a route that was obviously well known to them.

The path they took was not always the one that the terrain immediately suggested was the best way to get around or over an obstacle. But only once did the uniformed man query a decision made by the rider beside him: when Casey swung off to the side to go around an escarpment instead of heading down a ravine that cut into it.

'Been more than ten years since you were out this way?' the new sheriff said.

127

'A lot more, pal. Not since I was in school.'

England gave his first indication that he was familiar with the way to Twin Bluffs when he said: 'Rockfall blocked off the ravine a couple of years ago. After some big rains.'

It seemed somehow colder out in the country than in town, the mist of their own and the horses' expelled breath whiter and more dense. While the other three men continued to blow their lung-warmed air into cupped hands at frequent intervals, Willy Casey seemed almost impervious to the chill of the night. And began to talk in the same gabby way as when he and Edge had first met up over a bottle of rye whiskey in the Black Hat.

'About halfway to where we're headed now, Mr Edge. Won't see the two pieces of high ground for which the place is named until we're almost at them. On account of them being down in a valley that's pretty well hidden. Not too far from town.'

'Two and one third miles, pal,' Kemp put in. 'I recall we measured it out as a school project.'

'Sounds about right,' Casey allowed, and with a sideways glance and a tone of voice that showed he perhaps resented the interruption. Certainly he spoke more forcefully for a few moments, as if to challenge any other attempt to cut in on what he was saying. 'Guess most folks from Pomona have been out to Twin Bluffs once or twice. Maybe went there special for a church or Fourth of July picnic like they used to hold out there in the old days. Or when they was huntin'. Pretty good huntin' country all over these sections to the south of town. I used to be down here a lot of times . . . Back when I was ranchin'. Before I got the dead leg.'

Edge thought that Willy Casey was using talk to block out bad feelings that came to him when there was silence. But the nostalgic line he had been following suddenly went sour on him. For their own reasons, the cavalry corporal and the former sheriff of Pomona remained unconcerned about whether the lame man stayed quiet or continued to gab. For a good reason, as he maintained his habitual

surveillance of the surroundings, the half-breed brought
Casey out of the painful past and into a present of which
he was apprehensive.

'What makes you so sure the Comanche braves are out
this way, feller?'

'Uh?' He was startled out of a morose reverie. 'Yeah. It's
where they always run to when they blot their copybooks or
make enough money to buy some liquor.' He jerked a
thumb over his shoulder. 'Mr England has personal experience of that.'

The overweight man in the frock coat accepted the
invitation of the thin one in the ragged jacket. Explained:
'White Eagle and Black Hawk have their uses in Pomona.
They don't have any skills and they aren't too bright. But
they're strong and if you keep close watch on them they'll
work hard at any kind of manual chore. For a lot less than
people would have to pay a white man they hired on.'

'Indian scum,' Kemp murmured, and seemed startled
that he had spoken aloud what was in his mind.

'There'll be no shootin' by us unless they start in to
throw lead first!' Casey warned, his voice ice cold. And it
was apparent the threat of a potential gunfight was at the
root of his fear.

Edge guessed that they were drawing close to their
destination as they started to move up a rock-strewn incline
that rose in a gentle slope with just the cloudless, star-
pricked and moon-bright sky visible above the crest. This
made it likely that a hidden valley lay beyond the rise.
Also, the distance they had covered from Pomona seemed
to be about right. And the tension that had sounded
in Casey's commanding tones now infected Kemp and
England – could be seen in the sudden rigidity of the way
they sat their saddles.

England's tone remained the same, but he began to
speak faster. 'Anyway, for most of the time the Indians
did what work they could get and lived peacefully in
their squalid hovel across from the Papist church on Old

129

Pomona. Learned their lesson not to get drunk and cause trouble in town after my predecessor locked them up a few times. After that, the only problem he had with them – and then I had to handle it a couple of times – was when they stole. When there was no work for awhile and their need for a drink was too strong to resist. Then they'd steal the liquor or anything they thought they could sell to buy liquor.'

'And always scooted out here to get themselves drunk as skunks,' Casey came in on the explanation. 'And old Sheriff McCann, then Mr England here when he took on the lawman's job, always knew where to look for the crazy lunkheads.' He and Kemp reined in their mounts at the crest of the rise, and as Edge moved up alongside him and England halted beside the uniformed man, he announced: 'We're here.'

From immediately in front of them the ground fell away more steeply than it had been rising. And it dropped to a lower point, into a lushly grassed valley that inscribed a graceful arc from the west to the south east. The two steep-sided, perhaps sixty-feet high slabs of rock which gave the place its name were in the centre of the valley's bottom land, halfway around the curve. There was a gap of some three hundred feet between the bluffs and some tall, healthy-looking pines grew thick in this space. A short way back in the timber a small fire was alight, sending up a thin column of grey smoke that rose straight from out of the tree tops, and was not wafted away until it reached into the turbulent air currents that flowed across the gap between the rocks.

'Always came back as docile as beaten dogs,' England continued, reflectively as Casey clucked to his horse and signalled for them all to start down the slope that was not littered with loose rocks on this side of the rise. 'Long as they were given time to drink their fill and sleep some of it off. Liked to spend a couple of days in the cells out back of the law office. Had their three squares a day at the town's expense. Didn't so much like working off the debt they owed to whoever they'd stolen from. But they always did it.'

'Never did anythin' like this before,' Casey said as the riders in a line of four reached the grassy bottom of the grade and angled out to move along a direct route toward the timbered, canyon-like gap that separated the two almost identically formed dark-hued rocky crags.

'Indian scum are capable of about any evil deed it's possible for the human mind to conceive,' Kemp rasped. 'I've seen enough of what they've done in my army service to know that.'

'This ain't no army patrol, soldier,' Casey growled. 'This is law business. I'm the sheriff. And you ain't even been made a deputy. None of you have. On account of I know these Injuns and I don't reckon they'll cause no trouble.' He had to swallow hard to rid his throat of a constriction. 'Like me and Mr England been sayin', they never was big trouble in the past.'

'They never fired a gun at anything but the sky before, Willy,' England reminded ominously, fingering the scar on his chin. 'When they were happy drunk. They would have been stone cold sober when they shot the horses this afternoon.'

'I'm just tryin' to do my job like I reckon it oughta be done, Mr England,' Casey explained, defending himself, but firm in his belief that he was right. Then his tone hardened when he barked: 'That no shootin' first rule applies to you as well, mister!'

Edge had been blowing into his cupped right hand and when he was through he did not lower it as usual to take the reins from the left. Instead, responding to a warning from his sometimes reliable sixth sense for being watched, he fisted the breath-warmed hand around the cold metal frame of the booted Winchester. And spoke out of the side of his hardly moving mouth to the alarmed Casey:

'Guess it'll be okay to shoot back, feller?'

131

Kemp flipped open his holster flap. Murmured softly: 'I get that same itchy feeling, pal.'

England, reacting to their moves rather than to any form of the instinct that had triggered them, dropped a hand to grasp his own rifle in its rear-slung boot. Then, like the half-breed and the cavalryman, he checked the action of drawing the weapon. And peered in the same direction as them – into the moon-shadowed darkness beneath the trees, now less than a hundred yards away.

'You didn't try to stop them from coming, Willy,' he growled in low tones. 'And I reckon you're best advised to use them. A couple of men who know more about this kind of situation than a couple of amateur lawmen like us will ever . . .'

His voice tailed away as he now sensed what it was that had first aroused the suspicion of Edge and Kemp. Then knew for certain, just as they did, that the suspicion was well founded. There were watchers concealed there in the darkness under the trees. And they were not crouching there in trembling trepidation. There was hostility in those hidden eyes: and a resolution to do what had to be done to preserve what every man holds most dear – his life.

'Oh, my God!'

England rapped out the plea to the Almighty as two stabs of muzzle flame showed in the darkness a part of a second before the pair of reports sounded so close together they almost cracked out as one.

Edge thudded in his heels and yelled at the chestnut gelding to demand an instant gallop. Had the Winchester clear of the boot before his horse took a first lengthened stride. And fired a shot in unison with the angry snort that was the animal's protest at the cruel abruptness of the command.

Two more shots blasted out of the timber. And, like the opening pair, they were aimed at an angle that made the riders – not the horses – the targets. Edge crouched low in the saddle. Worked the lever action of the repeater one-handed to eject the spent shellcase and jack a fresh round into the breech. Felt the killer's grin spread over his lean face. An expression that narrowed his eyes to glittering threads and drew back his lips to display little more than the crack where his clenched teeth came together. A grin that had first involuntarily taken command of his features at times of kill or be killed when he had ridden into the bedlam battles of the War Between the States. And now, as he exploded a second shot at the unseen enemy, he was aware of a rider drawing level with him. A man in the familiar blue and yellow uniform of the United States Cavalry.

But he did not allow his mind to wander for more than an instant away from the dangerous present. In that part of a second perhaps became again a full captain of cavalry with absolute authority over a most junior non-com. Roared:

'Go right, Corporal!'

He triggered a third shot as he wrenched on the reins to angle his mount to the left. And his grin momentarily expressed something close to exhilaration as he saw Harry Kemp veer to the right. And heard the uniformed man's instinctive response to the command: 'Sir!'

Then Edge thrust the rifle back in the boot. Began to slow his mount. Heard and saw Kemp firing his Colt into the timber that was now less than fifty yards away. To the right and left side respectively of the half-breed and the trooper. While England and Casey, bringing up the rear, continued to gallop straight at the trees. England had his rifle drawn, but was still struggling to work its action after firing an opening shot. Casey needed both his hands to cling to the saddle of his racing horse.

Several seconds had elapsed since shots had exploded from out of the timber between the bluffs. But Edge and Kemp took no chances. As they closed with the fringe of the stand, sixty or so feet to either side of where the muzzle flashes had stabbed out of the blackness, they halted their

133

mounts and leapt from the saddles without wasting a moment. And dropped to their haunches in the cover of thorny brush and more solid pine trunks. Their horses moved sullenly away, breathing heavily and snorting.

Edge had drawn his Colt as he hit the grassy ground. Thumbed back the hammer. Felt far from exhilarated now as he watched England and Casey bring their horses to stand-stills, twenty yards back from the fringe of the pines. The former sheriff of Pomona aiming his Winchester from the shoulder. The newly-appointed lawman reaching across to draw and then aim the fancy revolver with the long barrel. Both men and their every move clearly illuminated in the hard light of the moon. For stretched seconds, Edge felt like every muscle in his body was pulled taut to breaking point as he listened for an explosive barrage of gunshots: rigidly poised to respond. To lunge forward, triggering a hail of bullets at the Comanches who would have blasted Casey and England out of their saddles.

But the lengthening silence continued to be marred only by the breathing of men and horses. Their breath vaporising in the winter night air; drifting for a shorter time than the acrid black powder smoke of the recent gunfire.

'You men all right?' Casey asked, his voice sounding almost painfully strained as he kept his attention riveted on the spot from which they had been fired on.

When the query failed to draw any responses, England looked toward Edge and Kemp. Then whispered something to Casey. Casey nodded, then remained in the saddle as England began to dismount. Still peering into the moon-shadowed trees and aiming the Colt in the same direction. But after that single nod, his attitude was too woodenly rigid to suggest he was covering England's dismount. Instead, he looked to be petrified: unable to move a muscle, no matter what happened. Until, a moment after England was on the ground, his gun hand sank to rest on the thigh of his dead leg, his chin dropped toward his chest and he toppled sideways out of his saddle. He was limp and unfeeling when he hit the ground and sprawled out half on his side and half on his face. His horse whinnied and shied away.

'Oh, my God, Willy's fainted,' England groaned. And dropped to one knee, reaching out a hand toward the sprawled man while he kept his rifle pointed into the trees and raked his gaze between the crouching forms of Edge and Kemp.

'So he ain't no damn use to us right now,' Edge murmured, not loud enough for anyone else to hear.

Then gunfire exploded again. From deeper in the timber. Maybe as far back as where the column of woodsmoke had revealed a campfire. Bullets crackled amongst the trees at a frenetic rate of fire. Thudding into trunks, ricocheting off them or whining out into the open unhindered. The barrage so intense it sounded like there were far more than two repeaters blazing potential death through the bitterly cold night.

England, caught out in the open, hurled himself hard to the ground: in a position that placed his bulky form between the gunfire and the helpless Casey. This as Edge and Kemp remained on their haunches, but with their backs pressed tight against the sturdy pine trunks that shielded them.

Tension stretched time, and then the abrupt silence that followed the sudden end to the cacophony of cracking gunshots and splintering wood seemed to have a brittle, palpable presence. Until Edge powered upright, swung around the covering tree and started to explode a fusillade of his own. Had blasted off two shots when Kemp matched his move. England used the barrage for cover: rose up on to all fours and scampered to the fringe of the trees. Triggered two rifle shots at unseen targets after the revolvers of the half-breed and the cavalryman had rattled empty. Then held his fire for more stretched seconds while just the sounds of the two men reloading their handguns kept utter silence at bay.

'I think that maybe –' England began to say in a husky whisper.

'Shut up!' Edge snarled, his head cocked to the side in an attitude of straining to hear sounds from a distance.

Simultaneously, Kemp demanded: 'Quit it, pal!'

Hoofbeats at the gallop. Thudding on soft ground. Never obtrusively loud and within moments diminishing.

'They're beating it!' Kemp groaned.

'Like on the way to the farm!' England said in much the same tone.

Edge had already started to run. And again the cavalryman followed his example. They reached the spot where England was getting to his feet. This was close to where a narrow pathway offered access through the thickly-growing timber. Where the path cut into the trees the moonlight glinted on the metal of more than just two ejected shellcases. To show that this was where the Comanches had been when they fired the opening shots.

The half-breed paused only for a moment, then started along the path. The other two were close on his heels. The eyes of all of them were now accustomed to the darkness – several degrees removed from pitch blackness – that filled the timber-crowded area between the two rocky bluffs. Then, some forty yards or so from the fringe of the stand of pines, they emerged into a clearing that was lit by the moon and the dully glowing embers of an almost burned-out fire. Here they came to an easy halt, England and Kemp moving up to flank Edge. And each of them lowered their guns as the tension drained out of their nervous systems. They began to breath normally again after what seemed to have been a very long time.

The Comanches were dead, their duster-coated forms sprawled out face down on the hard-packed, sparsely-grassed ground on opposite sides of the dying fire. It was not just the dark bloodstains blossomed on the backs of

136

their coats that told of their death. Nor the way their arms were outstretched, hands clawed, toward the rifles that had been hurled away as they took the bullets in the back and were pitched into death. For such attitudes could well have been posed, to play dead as a part of some table-turning trick. Indians were expert at faking death. But not even stone cold sober Comanches could have faked the total inertia of undeniable death that fixed these figures so unmovingly silent to the ground. And White Eagle and Black Hawk had not been sober when they died.

'Do you think . . .?' England started uneasily, not trusting the evidence of his eyes. And he levelled the rifle at his hip in a double-handed grip.

'No, they're dead,' Edge said, and looked at Kemp to ask: 'I guess that's your Pa's still, Corporal?'

The wood-framed, brass dingus for distilling corn mash into alcohol stood over to one side of the clearing, along with a heap of two saddles and bedrolls. Close by there were some bottles of a shape and colour familiar to Edge. A dozen or so, standing upright, stoppered and undoubtedly full. Near the fire and the corpse of the taller brave three empty bottles lay on their sides. And two others that were stoppered and half-full.

'Sure looks like it, pal,' Kemp replied with just a fleeting glance at the still before he returned his attention to the corpses. And there was a grin of evil pleasure on his broken-nosed face as he rasped: 'Well, what do you know? We got them on the run. We sure as hell did *get* them on the run. The redskinned scum!'

'And all the evidence that they killed your family is here,' England pointed out with a quieter degree of satisfaction.

'About Casey, feller,' Edge said.

England had been about to move toward the bodies. Suddenly checked his advance: and had to swallow hard before he could force out: 'Oh my God, Willy! I was going to tell you men – I think he was shot!'

137

'Poor sonofabitch,' Kemp said evenly, shaking his head and pushing the revolver back in his holster as the final traces of pleasure left his face.

'I don't know,' England qualified. And seemed at a loss. 'At first I thought he passed out, but . . .'

'Let's go check on him, pal,' Kemp offered. Then, in the same tone to Edge: 'I'll round up our horses?' He peered into the darkness beneath the pines on the far side of the clearing. 'Don't reckon there's a chance of us finding the ones that bolted tonight.'

'Sure, Corporal,' Edge said dismissively as he holstered his Colt. 'I'll take care of what needs to be done here.'

'Appreciate it, pal. Dead as they are, if I'm left alone with that scum, there's no telling what I'm liable to do to them. Now I've got used to seeing them dead, I can't get it out of my mind what they did to my parents and sister.'

'Sure, Corporal,' Edge said again, his manner distant as he moved toward the corpses flanking the fire.

'Let's go,' England urged. Eager to check on Willy Casey but seemingly reluctant to do so alone.

And now Kemp was suddenly torn between a desire to leave the clearing and a compulsion to remain. He eyed the half-breed suspiciously, like he did not trust Edge to do what he had said, plain and simple. But then he shook his head with an emphatic gesture and this seemed to clear his mind of the doubt. And he made the first move back along the path between the pines.

Edge crossed to pick up an unopened bottle of Donald Kemp's high quality firewater. Took a hefty slug from the neck and swilled it around in his mouth as he returned to the centre of the clearing. Then he spat it into the fire and it hissed briefly among the hot ashes. He found that the bad taste that the small skirmish had left in his throat was gone with the spit and he tilted the bottle again. This time swallowed the fine-tasting liquor. It required an effort to ration himself to the one drink. But this is what he did, and then carried out a brief search of the campsite: twice needing to strike matches to supplement the light of the moon. Having seen as much as he needed, he next wrapped the corpses in their own blankets and bound them with lengths of rope cut from one of their lariats. He was about to light a fresh-rolled cigarette when England and Kemp returned to the clearing, each of them leading two horses. The corpse of Willy Casey was blanket-wrapped and draped over the saddle on his own gelding.

'He didn't just pass out,' the uniformed man reported unnecessarily, after directing a baleful glare at the bodies of the Comanches, tightly bound in the improvised shrouds.

'You made a neater job with them than I did with Willy,' England said morosely. And fingered his moustache while his thumb traced back and forth along the line of the scar on his chin.

'Maybe because I've had more experience of taking care of the new dead, feller,' Edge answered. He tossed the match among the ashes and its brief flame was all that was alight. 'And how they get to be dead. You should take a look at –'

'Willy was shot in the chest,' the big-framed man in the too tight frockcoat broke in, his tone still appropriately funereal. 'Came out of it long enough to do a little talking. You recall how he was so eager that we shouldn't fire first? Seems he didn't want to start a gunfight . . . in case he wouldn't be able to take care of his fair share. In the event, it was one of the first shots the Indians fired that hit him. Came within a half inch of going into his heart and killing him stone dead right off, I'd say.'

Kemp had traded a knowing glance with Edge soon after the man began his plaintive but determined lamentation. A glance that expressed tacit agreement to allow England the opportunity to finish what he felt he needed to say. Then they had started in on the final preparations to leave the campsite in the clearing. While the one-time sheriff of Pomona, seemingly withdrawn into a private world

139

removed from the unhurried activity, continued to say his piece about his dead successor.

'Said to thank you again for shooting the gun away from that woman who was fixing to kill him back in town, Mr Edge. And not to think it was a wasted bullet because either White Eagle or Black Hawk was set to kill him later anyway. Had the chance to show those sonsofbitches that he could be more than just a drunken cripple!'

Anger had suddenly replaced sadness, in his tone and his dark eyes. And both Edge and Kemp interrupted their chore of draping a dead Comanche over the horse alongside the corpse of Casey as they realised this was the first time they had heard Larry England curse. And perhaps it was this same realisation that shook the man out of his state of detachment. After which, he looked quickly from Kemp to Edge and then raked his gaze over the clearing. Then, as impassive as Edge, he asked evenly:

'About ready to leave?'

'Don't want to over-burden any of the horses,' Kemp said. 'We'll leave the still and bottles. And the other Indian.'

'Fine about the still and bottles, soldier. I'll carry the second Comanche on my mount.' He sounded fully composed now, and there was even a commanding manner about the way he moved toward the corpse still on the ground and looked pointedly over his shoulder for help. 'I want the people of Pomona to see all at one time just what kind of havoc they caused when they tried to sweep their dirt under the carpet.'

'Sure thing, pal,' Kemp agreed enthusiastically. Moved to lend a hand.

Within a few minutes, they were ready to leave Twin Bluffs. And by his own choice England, who had one corpse securely tied behind his saddle also took up the lead line on Casey's mount that was doubly-draped with limp, blanket-shrouded bodies. He said pointedly:

'You men sure aren't over-burdening your mounts with

140

that bottle apiece of evidence I saw you stash in your saddlebags.'

'Plenty more evidence left here, pal,' the scowling cavalryman countered with a wave of an arm to encompass the campsite. And with his bitterness drawing close to an explosion of rage, he added: 'Maybe it's even better the fine folks of the fine town of Pomona should come out here to see the evidence in the place where we . . .'

He slammed a fist into an open palm as the rising anger thickened his voice to an extent where no more words were able to squeeze up through his throat.

Edge drawled: 'Speaking of evidence, feller –'

'You're right, soldier,' England agreed emphatically. 'You had a hand in seeing that the killers of your family paid the price. No reason for you to want anything else. Except maybe a drink or two if you're so minded. Same as you, Edge. Now that no one can seriously accuse you of the lynchings, it's over. And me, I'm not the town sheriff anymore. The finer points of the law don't concern me. Way I feel fight now, all I want to do is rub the noses of Pomona people in the mess of Willy Casey's death.'

He shared a questioning look between Kemp and Edge as he finished. The cavalry corporal nodded in response to this. Edge drawled wearily:

'Right now, feller, I guess you could say I'm too dog tired to argue about that kind of crap.'

141

Eleven

LARRY ENGLAND had looked ready to react in a fury to
Edge's soft-spoken insult. But then Harry Kemp had defused the tension with a platitude about everyone being a
little over-wrought after their brush with death.

Then they made the start of the return to town. Rode
in single file without speaking for a long time through
the brightly moonlit, bitingly chill night. The grim-faced
moustached man leading the way, with the seemingly
contented cavalry non-com following behind the corpse-
draped horse and the impassively vigilant half-breed bringing up the rear. Then England turned in his saddle and
leaned slightly to the side to look beyond Kemp at Edge.
Offered contritely to both the men:

'I was out of line, telling you how you should be
after what's happened. It's been a rough day. We made
allowances for Corporal Kemp earlier so –'

'What I said, pal,' Kemp growled. 'Back there. Rough
day for all of us.'

'Even so . . .'

'No sweat, feller,' Edge filled in the pause after England
dried up.

'Thanks,' the man at the head of the line acknowledged.
And then felt sufficiently unburdened of guilt to bite off a
chew of tobacco.

After this an infrequent spit of juice at the ground
was the only sound made by any of the riders of the

slow-moving horses. Until they were back on the trail and close enough to town to see the buildings. When it was Harry Kemp who felt the need to speak, as England got rid of the chewed-out wad of tobacco with a louder than usual spit – that perhaps revealed his present feelings for the citizens of Pomona.

'Sure seems quiet,' the cavalryman said in a hushed whisper, as if he felt an involuntary compulsion to respect the peace of the town.

'Most people will be at church,' England explained flatly. 'Reverend Webster always holds a Thanksgiving service before the annual supper.'

'They won't be giving us any thanks for what we're bringing to town tonight,' Kemp muttered with sneering vindictiveness.

'And I guess some of them will lose their appetites for the turkey and cranberry sauce,' England added tautly. 'After I make them admit they're as much to blame for Willy being dead as the Comanches.'

They advanced on to the start of Old Pomona and the uniformed man urged his horse forward so that he rode beside England. While Edge remained at the rear as they moved between the adobe buildings that flanked the narrow street: like he had set himself apart from whatever it was the other two men intended to do in town.

In fact, he was pre-occupied for another few moments with his motives for returning to Pomona with these men who had unfinished business here. Had needed to think along this line, since Larry England had called it right. It was over for him, in terms of being free to ride away from this west Texas town without anyone here doubting his innocence of the Kemp lynchings. But, he had now concluded at the end of several minutes of introspection, he could not yet leave without regarding himself as guilty of something else.

The group of three living men and three dead ones kept on going past the funeral parlour of Otis Boone where the corpses would eventually be deposited for preparations for their burial. Then, further up the street, they rode by the mean adobe shack in which the two Comanches had lived in squalor. Directly across from the shack, the dim and flickering light of candles showed from in the depths of the Catholic church. It was the only glimmer of light visible along the entire length of Old Pomona and it was just possible for the riders to discern the muted droning sounds of a number of voices in prayer. No more than a dozen.

'Father O'Donnell holds a service each Thanksgiving, too,' England explained. 'There aren't many Papists in Pomona. They'll all get together with the others for the supper later.'

Even before they reached the intersection of Old Pomona with Main Street they could hear a larger congregation in the Episcopalian church, their voices raised in the singing of a hymn that almost drowned out the accompanying pump organ. The hymn came to the kind of abrupt end that is usually a feature of sacred music as the riders swung around the stand of stunted pines in the fork of the streets. And the clop of hooves on the hard-packed ground sounded suddenly much louder as they advanced on the stone church that spilled bright lamplight out of several of its windows. But the arched entrance was in shadows, so the door was firmly closed and when massed voices began to intone a prayer this made it even less likely that the worshippers would hear any but the loudest of disturbances from outside.

And, apart from the unobtrusive noise of the horses' unhurried progress, the only other sounds were of England and Kemp in low-voiced conversation and the footfalls of Mrs Cloris Snelling as she made another diagonal crossing of the street between the Rio Grande boarding house and the graveyard beside the church.

Then the frockcoated man and the uniformed non-com made sounds and gestures of reaching agreement and angled off the centre of the street to head for the meeting

144

hall directly opposite the church. The meeting hall was the only other building along the entire length of Main to be lit. Only when the two men reined their mounts to a halt did they become aware that Edge had not followed them.

'Hey, pal, don't you want to –' Kemp began. His voice was still pitched low, but the tone was conspiratorial now.

The half-breed made to break in on the cavalryman, but England spoke first:

'He's right to figure this part is none of his business,' the former sheriff of Pomona said, addressing Kemp but directing a quizzical look at the half-breed.

Edge acknowledged the truth of England's assumption with a forefinger touched to the brim of his hat. Then continued to ride on up the street as the other two dismounted.

Seemingly totally withdrawn into her private world of grief, the mourning-garbed Cloris Snelling entered the cemetery. And she was still there, standing unmoving and silent beside one of the many-times scarred tombstones, ten minutes or so later. When Edge went into the burial ground beside the church with its low wall, after bedding down his chestnut gelding in the livery stable. She turned her head to watch him approach from several yards away. Her face was concealed behind the black veil, but there was no abruptness in the slight movement to suggest he had startled her. And her even tone of voice was further proof of this when she said:

'Three more dead. I saw you and the others bring them in.'

She turned her head a little more, to look away from Edge and toward the front of the meeting hall. Where the horses of England and Kemp and Casey stood in quiet docility, their saddles empty of both living and dead. Just the voice of the Reverend Alvin Webster rang out from the Episcopalian church now, his words indistinct but his tone unmistakably that of a parson preaching a sermon.

Now the bereaved woman did snap her head around

with a jerk – reacting to the flare of the match Edge had struck on the butt of Frontier Colt that jutted out from under the rucked-up hem of his sheepskin coat. She saw that there was a fresh-made cigarette angled from a side of his mouth, but before he moved the match to light it he first used its flame to illuminate the small marker of white marble on the grave that was humped between them. The inscription, ravaged by the elements, read:

In
memory of
Joy
daughter of
Elroy and Cloris Snelling
Died aged
seven

The date of the little girl's death was ten years in the past.

'Is your curiosity satisfied, sir?' the woman asked and there was just a trace of resentment in her cultured voice.

'Ten years is a long time to stay in mourning, Mrs Snelling,' he replied as he shook out the match and tossed it toward a neglected grave with a leaning marker.

'It strikes me as unlikely that you ever had and tragically lost a child, sir,' she countered, with no hint of any kind of rancour now.

Edge almost responded with anger to her presumption. This as her words triggered vivid images of Conchita Lopez into his mind. This at the end of the first day in very many when he had been able to block such painful recollections out of his awareness. But, of course, the mother of the small girl buried in this grave was absolutely right. He never had fathered a daughter.

'But it is not for my little girl that I am in deep mourning,' the woman augmented as she shifted her veiled gaze away

146

from the impassive face of the half-breed to peer down at the marker with the small bunch of colourful flowers at its base. 'Come tomorrow it will be two weeks that Elroy has been dead.'

'Not here in Pomona? Unless you couldn't stay alone in the house and moved into –'

'Don't you know?' she broke in, perturbed rather than surprised.

'Willy Casey started to tell me, ma'am. We got sidetracked, as I remember.'

She did not respond for several moments. And seemed at ease with her thoughts. The parson's voice droned on. Larry England emerged from the meeting hall and took up the reins of all three horses to lead them down an alley between the hall and the feed and grain store. The man, hatless but still wearing the frockcoat with strained buttons directed a surreptitious glance toward the church. But he gave no sign that he saw the couple in the cemetery beside it.

'Why do you find me interesting, sir?' Cloris Snelling asked at length. And despite the fine mesh veil that even bright sunlight could not have penetrated, Edge felt he was able to visualise her expression. The woman was only mildly intrigued – like she was ninety-nine percent certain she knew how he would reply.

'I didn't know why I should be when Casey started to tell me, ma'am. He was just a drunk panhandling drinks at the time. But one of the dead Comanches lived long enough to finger write a few letters in the dust. Just an S and an N and an E and one L. He was pretty close to his Happy Hunting Ground and maybe he wasn't the neatest hand at lettering when he was fit and well, but –'

'I never intended for anyone to be killed, sir,' she cut in, not insistently. But she knew she did not have to be overly assertive as she once again shifted her veiled gaze from heavily-bristled, hat-brim-shadowed face of Edge to the moonlit grave. 'I attempted only to ensure that

147

those responsible for the lynching of the Kemps escaped punishment.'

She sucked in a deep breath from the chill night air and Edge checked the impulse to interject an ironic comment. Because he felt suddenly certain that this woman was at present incapable of any form of subterfuge. That, standing here beside the grave of her long dead daughter, she was even eager to expunge her guilt with the truth.

'It seemed absolutely right that the Kemps should be put to death in the way they were,' she continued after expelling the breath in a long sigh. Her tone was resolute, and although he had never seen her undoubtedly fleshy face he conjured up a picture of her mouth set in a taut, grudgeful line. 'When you and the son came to Pomona to tell of what happened at the farm, I felt little short of elated, sir. But then I learned the sheriff intended to carry out a thorough investigation of the crime. And it troubled me that somebody could well be penalised for carrying out an action that Elroy and I should have undertaken.'

She had started to drywash her black gloved hands with increasing intensity. Now realised what she was doing. And dropped her arms loosely to her sides. She also moderated her voice that had started to become a little shrill. She gestured with her head toward a far corner of the cemetery and went on:

'The Indians were engaged in some repairs of the boundary wall over there. For a dollar each they were more than eager to do my bidding, sir. But I instructed them to raze the Kemp farm to the ground. No more nor less. I understand they set up an ambush in which you and the sheriff and the Kemp boy could well have been killed?'

She looked at Edge, her head rigid on her shoulders. This attitude sufficient to convey the brand of sincerity that would be fixed upon her veiled features.

'Ended with a couple of horses dead, ma'am,' the half-breed said.

She nodded. 'I can only think they were late in leaving

148

town to go to the farm and needed to delay you and the others.'

'Never know for sure now.'

She sighed again, and her stance and voice exuded sadness as she gazed down at the grave. Just as the congregation in the nearby church entered into a responsive prayer with the parson. 'I suppose I should have realised the temptation of the strong drink at the Kemp farm would have been too strong for the Indians to resist. I heard that Mr Sinclair from the Black Hat Saloon had overheard your plans to ride out to Twin Bluffs and confront the Indians. But I never for one moment thought you would kill the wretched creatures.'

'Ain't so sure we did, ma'am,' Edge said.

'What?' she demanded with another jerked motion of her head to signal her shock.

He did not answer for a few stretched seconds, during which it was as if he tried to penetrate the veil with the powerful stare of the glinting slits of his narrowed eyes beneath their hooded lids. Then he told her: 'I don't think that concerns you right now, Mrs Snelling. What interests me is why you were so happy that the Kemps were lynched? Unless your husband maybe died a drunk from drinking too much of Donald Kemp's –'

'Elroy never touched hard liquor in his life!' the widow snapped. And again had to make a conscious effort to tighten a grip on composure. 'And in any event had scant opportunity to drink that moonshine in the past decade, sir. Since we left Pomona soon after our daughter was killed. And visited the town just once a year on the anniversary of her death. Elroy died in El Paso of the effects of pneumonia aggravating the consumption that plagued him for the last two years of his life.'

Edge could sense her eyes staring fixedly at his face, tacitly demanding a sympathetic apology. Instead, on a small stream of expelled tobacco smoke, he said: 'The Kemps killed your daughter, Mrs Snelling?'

For a few moments it seemed that the woman was either going to demand some degree of emotional involvement from the impassive half-breed, or swing around and stride away from him. But the aggression drained out of her as she began to relive the tragic events of so many years ago. 'We ran the boarding house then. When we were busy, there was little time to spare for Joy. She liked to go out and stay with the Kemps on school vacations. They thought a great deal of her and treated her as one of their own. Elroy and I never thought badly of them for their Dunker faith. Even respected them for having the courage to stick by their pacifist views. And Edwina and Donald Kemp had our sympathy for how their boy was so dead set on joining the army. Then went off and did just that.'

The service in the Episcopalian church was ended and the large congregation was at its noisiest as the people began to leave.

'But then the Kemp place was raided by a band of Apache Indians, sir. While our daughter was staying on the farm. The Kemps all freely admitted it. Not Donald nor Edwina nor Anna raised a hand against the attackers. Stood by and watched, even when the savages abducted little Joy. A seven-year-old child incapable of defending herself. All the Kemps did was come to town to tell us what had happened.'

The smaller group of Pomona citizens that had been in the Catholic church started up Main to merge with the people streaming directly across the street toward the meeting hall. There was a great deal of laughter as everyone shed their mood of reverence and prepared for the enjoyment to come.

'The entire town turned out to search for little Joy,' Mrs Cloris Snelling went on, giving no sign that she was aware of the happily noisy throng on the street. 'She was found within an hour of us starting out from the Kemp farm to look for her. In a ravine. Stripped of every article of her

150

clothing. Terribly mutilated. Quite obviously she had been –'

'I'm obliged, ma'am,' Edge broke in on the woman who was still speaking in a calm, rational manner.

But perhaps she was too composed, he thought. Maybe the strain of keeping a grip on her emotions would prove too much and she might suddenly break down. But he was wrong.

'Thank you, sir. After such a long time I can think of her and talk of her in that condition without becoming hysterical. But thank you for not . . .' She sighed and gave a slight shrug. 'I agree, it would serve no purpose to go into the details. Elroy and I began to hate the Kemps. To such an extent that we realised we might not have been able to keep ourselves from punishing them – for not even trying to protect our little girl. That was why we moved away to El Paso. And only returned to Pomona on the anniversary of Joy's awful death. Over the years our feelings toward the Kemps became less powerful. Just as the feelings of our fellow townspeople did. Perhaps because we realised that the passing of time could not nullify the guilt the Kemps suffered? Surely there is no kind of religious faith that can hold people immune from –'

She broke off, made suddenly aware of the crowd on the street. This as a man in the meeting hall doorway roared:

'What the friggin' hell?' His voice cut across and then silenced the clamour of eager anticipation. 'You men must be crazy!'

It was the tall and skinny Jake Driscoll. His liver-spotted face expressed shock as he turned from the threshold of the hall to rake his gaze over the crowd of curious people. Then he showed relief when he saw the man he was looking for. And Ralph Lasky began to force a way through from the centre of the throng, voicing the demand that was in the mind of everyone:

'What's wrong, Jake?'

The silver-haired Brad Harrison was at the front of the crowd, and found himself unable to check the compulsion to see what it was that had shaken Driscoll. And the man, blinking rapidly and with the nervous tic constantly working his mouth, needed to take just two paces to peer in through the doorway. Gasped, swung around and needed to clutch at a door jamb to keep from swaying.

'It's Casey!' he reported shrilly. 'And the two Indians!' He seemed blind to the short and fat Ralph Lasky who came to a halt between him and Driscoll. 'They're all sitting at the councilmen's table! They look . . . I'm sure they're . . .'

'They're dead!' Lasky snarled. 'What's the idea?'

He made the demand against a sudden burst of talk that was triggered by his revelation. Then the noise subsided as he, Driscoll and Harrison retreated from the threshold of the meeting hall. And England and Kemp stepped into view from within the building to take their place in the doorway.

'Want for everyone in this town to come inside and take a look!' the former lawman announced grimly. 'To see that justice has been done in the matter of the murders at the Kemp farm. Want you to see, too, that all it cost was the life of a crippled drunk who you all thought was a joke. Come one, come all! No admission charge to take a look!

He half turned as he raised his voice to make the invitation. And made an elaborate gesture with his arms: ushering the people inside. This while Harry Kemp remained resolutely unmoving at his side, a challenging scowl on his dark-eyed, broken-nosed face.

A swell of murmuring talk began among the crowd. At first the tenor was questioning. But then an odd tone of angry non-comprehension was discernible. Until sudden silence was brought to the street again, when Mrs Snelling shouted:

'No!'

She was still standing beside the grave of her long-dead

152

daughter when she spoke the shrill denial. Then, as everyone turned toward her, she hurried past Edge to go to the gateway in the cemetery wall. Halted just beyond it and continued without stridency:

'You're wrong to place blame with the people of Pomona, sir. I am responsible for the killings!'

'Nonsense, Mrs Snelling!' Lasky argued.

Edge moved out through the gateway to stand beside the mourning-garbed widow.

'Cloris Snelling?' Harry Kemp asked doubtfully, the challenging scowl swept off his features by an expression of anguished understanding.

'Yes, son. That's who I am. And I paid the Indians to –'

'Then I'm going to have to kill you, lady!' the cavalryman snarled. And started to claw the revolver out of his holster.

The crowd split suddenly into two, the shocked and frightened people panicked into opening up a ten-feet-wide gap. So that no-one stood between the young man in the blue and gold uniform and the older woman in solid black. Until Edge stepped in front of Mrs Snelling. Stood squarely facing the man who had taken a step away from the threshold of the meeting hall as he got the Army Colt clear of the holster.

'This is no more your business, pal,' Kemp reminded as he hesitated, then kept on coming across the street. Moving between the two groups of people who were attired in their smartest outfits for the church service and Thanksgiving supper – none of them carrying a weapon.

Edge stood with his feet splayed a little, his left hand hanging loosely at his side while his right was slightly curled and raised to be close to the jutting butt of his revolver. The cigarette, wisping smoke, bobbed at the side of his mouth as he spoke:

'You better kill me soon as the range is right, Corporal.'

'Look, Mrs Snelling had nothing –' Otis Boone started to say.

'Shut up!' Driscoll snarled.

Kemp halted. Midway across the street and just clear of the gap that divided the crowd in two.

'Soldier, my gun's aimed at you!' Larry England warned. And began to close on Kemp from the rear, his Remington cocked and levelled.

Kemp ignored everyone except the half-breed as he said coolly: 'If I get killed doing what I have to do, I figure it'll be for the best, pal.'

He started to bring his gun hand up as he took another pace forward. The woman behind Edge caught her breath as the half-breed fisted his right hand to the butt of his revolver and drawled evenly:

'Figure you've got two more feet of ground to cover, Corporal. After that, one of us will pretty soon be covered by about six feet of it.'

'No!' the Pomona mayor roared. And it was the power of Lasky's voice rather than Edge's ominous threat that caused Harry Kemp to freeze as he was about to take his next fateful step toward the half-breed and the woman in black. 'Enough is enough! There will be no more slaughter because of the execution of the Kemp family!'

The expression of grim determination to accept Edge's challenge slowly slid off the face of Harry Kemp. And was replaced by a different brand of anguish to that which he had endured a few moments earlier. This as he turned slowly to put his back toward the half-breed and Mrs Snelling. And peered at the earnestly frowning Ralph Lasky as he attempted no resistance when the tense England took a final step and plucked the Army Colt out of his suddenly trembling hand.

'Execution?' the cavalry corporal questioned in a husky whisper.

People swallowed hard, gasped, sighed and cursed softly: variously expressing their sense of relief that the explosive situation had been defused. And then a different brand of tension began to mount as Kemp shifted his head

154

from side to side, his dark eyes demanding an answer from every face that his gaze swept over. But few of the smartly attired citizens of Pomona knew what was asked of them. Until Ralph Lasky recaptured massed attention when he said:

'That's right, soldier boy. Ten years to the day after they took no hand in attempting to prevent the killing of Joy Snelling. They were tried, found guilty and sentenced to be hanged.'

England blurted: 'Oh, my God!'

'Sonofabitch,' Kemp whispered forcefully.

And this signalled a burst of shocked talk that rose in volume until it was much louder than when this same throng of people had streamed out of the church to head across to the meeting hall.

Cloris Snelling was as stunned as anybody by the mayor's revelation. She reached out to touch Edge's arm and asked as he moved aside and turned to look quizzically at her: 'The Kemps were put on trial?'

'Seems so, ma'am.'

'But there's no court in Pomona. No one has legal . . . They had no right.'

The half-breed dropped his cigarette butt and crushed out its glowing embers under a boot heel.

'I knew nothing of this.'

'Neither did a lot of other people, I figure,' Edge said as the volume of talk diminished.

'It must have been a secret trial,' the widow murmured. 'Held in camera.'

The tall, lean, impassive-faced man at her side gestured across the street as he answered: 'Looks like Lasky's about to put everyone in the picture.'

155

Twelve

THE STORY of how Donald, Edwina and Anna Kemp came to be hanged from a branch of the leafless oak in the yard out front of their farm took just a few minutes for Ralph Lasky to tell.

For ten years the townspeople had experienced a sense of guilt about allowing the Dunker family to live on normally at their farm, just as if the tragedy of little Joy Snelling's death had never happened. But with the passing of time, the sharpness of the bad feeling had dulled. Until this tenth anniversary visit to town by the murdered girl's mother. When it became known that Cloris Snelling was a new widow. Which aroused in the minds of some people certain thoughts about the injustice of the situation – that while this woman had suffered so much, the Kemps were living a full and happy life on their fine farm in the country.

A number of citizens had voiced their thoughts, but it amounted only to empty talk. Until a special meeting of the town council was convened. A meeting that developed into the improvised trial at which it was unanimously decided to hang the Kemps. Three men were selected by the drawing of straws to carry out the execution. And only those who drew the short straws knew who they were. For the draw was made in secret and the men destined to go out to the Kemp place did so surreptitiously in the early hours of the morning.

So it was done. And Mrs Snelling – along with everyone

156

else not at the meeting of the council – had no knowledge of the secret trial and the carrying out of the sentence. Nor would the truth ever have been circulated had not a saddletramp and the returned-home Harry Kemp met up at the farm and later persuaded the Pomona sheriff to investigate the hangings.

Something over an hour after Ralph Lasky was through, and his fellow citizens had given their first tentative approval of the councilmen's actions, Edge and Harry Kemp were seated on one of the benches adjacent to the cannon plinth in the town park. They were sharing the bottle of corn liquor that the cavalryman had filched from the stock stolen by the two Comanches. Passing it back and forth and drinking without talking for some time they listened to the chatter and clatter from the meeting hall diagonally across the street. Each of them knowing it was not yet over. And each waiting for the other to broach the subject of their guilty knowledge.

'They sound to you like they're getting happier, pal?' Kemp asked at length in a neutral tone, with a negligent wave of a hand toward the brightly-lit building out of which the sounds of enjoyment spilled.

'It's Thanksgiving, feller. A happy time. And I guess a whole lot of Pomona people are giving thanks on the side to their council – for getting rid of their guilt for –'

'Yeah,' Kemp said, bitterness in his voice now. He took a deep swallow from the bottle, and as he thrust it toward Edge he asked: 'You knew there was something wrong with the set-up out at Twin Bluffs, didn't you?'

Lasky had admitted that two of the councilmen had gone out to where the Comanches were camped. Soon after Joe Sinclair had reported what he overheard in the saloon. The intention had been to make it appear that the Indians had died in a gunfight with England, Casey, Kemp and Edge. For dead Comanches would not be able to deny they killed the Kemps.

157

'They were both backshot in pretty much the same place,' Edge said. 'Seemed a little too neat and tidy. Way we were all just blasting blind through the timber. Then I saw sign that four horses were in the clearing recently. And the way that one of the braves tried to spell out the widow's name made it look like there was a double cross.'

'Wonder which of Lasky's bunch did it?'

'I don't give a damn, feller,' Edge answered and handed back the bottle without taking a drink.

And there was a sudden burst of louder noise from the meeting hall, as the door opened and Blanche Crabbe came out into the cold night. She carried a plate in each hand and hurried across the street with them.

'Here's some turkey for you men,' the elderly, emaciatedly thin owner of the candy store said quickly. 'Seein' as how you don't feel you oughta join us in the celebratin'.'

'Obliged, ma'am,' Edge said and took one of the proffered plates.

'It's cold now. But it was only a minute ago Larry England thought to send you out somethin' to eat. He's been made the town sheriff again.'

Kemp had been taking another long drink from the bottle and he ignored the plate of meat held out toward him. Then he belched and growled: 'I don't want anything from this lousy town, lady. Had my damn fill of it.'

Blanche Crabbe, dressed only in a thin gown, shivered as she responded sourly: 'So suit yourself, son!'

Then she spun around and hurried back across the street. Where, once again, the sounds of a crowd of people enjoying themselves were briefly much louder while the door of the meeting hall was open.

Edge had begun to eat some of the meat, and now shook his head to decline the offer of another drink from Kemp's bottle.

'So you can go to hell, along with everyone else in this stinking town!' the uniformed man muttered sullenly.

'When I'm done with living, and if there's such a place

as hell, then that's where I'll go, I guess.' He ate another piece of turkey as the man beside him sucked more liquor from the bottle that was almost empty. And Kemp still had the bottle tilted to his mouth when Edge asked evenly: 'You killed that kid, didn't you, Corporal?'

Kemp became rigid in the attitude of drinking from the neck of the bottle. Held the pose for perhaps three seconds. Then removed his tongue from where it had blocked the liquor from entering his mouth. Drained the bottle and opened his hand so that it slipped out of his grip, bounced off his thighs and landed on the ground. It did not break. He placed his hand on the bench at his side and lowered his head from the tilt. Stared straight out across the street, his expression seen in profile suggesting he was thinking deeply about how to answer the half-breed's query.

'Who said I did?' he asked at length. And seemed just mildly interested in what kind of response this might draw.

'Nobody, feller. Thought about the coincidence of you leaving the farm to enlist in the army ten years ago. About the same time the girl was killed. Also got to thinking about why a raiding party of renegade Indians just abducted the kid. When your folks didn't put up a fight. Seems to me they would have stolen some stuff. Done some damage. And your mother and sister would have served their purpose better than a seven year old kid.'

Kemp turned his head slowly, to gaze fixedly at Edge across three feet of brightly moonlit space. Full face, his expression was close to contentment. Then he nodded once, and returned his attention to the middle distance before he spoke.

'It was a piece of craziness, pal. I'd been having a lot of arguments with my parents on account of wanting to enlist in the cavalry. It was getting me down.' He looked at the bottle on the ground and touched it with a toe of his boot. 'I stole a bottle of the corn liquor and went up over the hill behind the orchards. I wasn't any kind of drinker in those days. Was drunk after three or four swallows.'

159

'Little Joy Snelling happened by. Collecting pebbles, I recall. She was a cute little kid. I liked her a lot. But just as a little kid . . . Until then. She laughed at me being drunk. Said she'd tell on me to my parents if I didn't give her a taste of the stuff. She snatched the bottle. I snatched it back. We started in to wrestle . . .'

He shook his head and gulped. 'Like I say, a piece of craziness. Sonofabitch, a seven year old girl . . . I never made it with her, pal. But I had to kill her because I'd tried to. She'd tell on me and I'd be lynched. I killed her with my bare hands . . . Then I cut her some . . . To hide the marks I'd made when I tried to . . .

'Anna found me when I was doing that. I hadn't even known the kid was screaming when it started. Loud enough for my sister to hear and come running. Hell of a thing, uh pal?'

'Your folks dreamed up the story about the renegade Indians?'

'Yeah. They told me that's what they were going to do. After they'd sent me away. To enlist. Everyone around Pomona knew it was what I wanted to do. And I hadn't been to town in over a week. So it held up.

'I knew it had held up, even though my folks never wrote me and I never came back until this morning. Because if it hadn't, I'd have been easy enough to find through the army.'

'Sure,' Edge said.

'You know why I did come back, pal?'

'I don't know anything about this, Corporal. You're telling me.' He chewed on some cold meat.

'Was going to confess. It's ten years to the day, just like Ralph Lasky said. And that was enough time for me to know that I'd never get free of the guilt. Was going to tell my folks what I planned to do. Then I was going to come on into town and do it, pal. But when I found them strung up like that . . . My father and mother and sister . . . Well, I just had to find out first who did that to them.'

160

'You had to figure it had a connection with the kid's killing?'

'Sure. And that made me feel even worse about it, pal. Because my folks had been lynched for protecting me. Time to go tell the people of this town about that now. Intended to . . . Wasn't anything you said.'

'Luck to you, Corporal,' Edge said as the cavalryman rose from the bench.

'Now we both know I only deserve the bad kind, pal.'

He started to move away, gaze fixed upon the meeting hall. And Edge started to chew on one final piece of meat before he set the still laden plate down on the bench where Kemp had sat.

Then a rifle shot cracked out. From around the side of the plinth. The bullet took the cavalry corporal in the centre of the back and sent him pitching heavily to the ground. Edge went down of his own volition – hurled himself off the end of the bench at the opposite side of the plinth from where the shot had come. Started to choke on a piece of meat that was caught in his throat. But did not make enough noise to drown out the sound of the rifle's repeater action being worked.

A second shot exploded another bullet into Harry Kemp's back as Edge coughed desperately to try to dislodge the blockage in his windpipe.

Then the familiar black-garbed form of Mrs Cloris Snelling stepped into view, her face still hidden by the veil. She ignored the half-breed and took four purposeful strides until she reached the side of the inert, spreadeagled body of Harry Kemp. Then worked the lever action once more, pressed the muzzle of the Winchester against the back of the trooper's head and squeezed the trigger a third time.

The head jerked and a spray of blood and fragments of bone splashed out of the exit wound in Kemp's face and soaked into the winter grass beneath it.

There had been a stunned silence in the meeting hall after the opening shot had sharply curtailed the chatter

161

and laughter. Now voices were raised in a vastly different tone. And footfalls thudded hollowly on floorboards. Chairs crashed over and some china and glass shattered.

'I'm sorry I startled you so, sir,' Mrs Snelling apologised dully from behind her veil. 'I just could not contain myself any longer.'

Edge coughed again, more forcefully. And the piece of meat was ejected out of his throat and into his mouth.

'The killer of my child is dead,' the widow went on. 'I thank you for doing what you said you would do. And for the loan of your rifle. Are you all right?'

The half-breed had risen to his feet. Now took the Winchester from the woman as she turned away from the bullet-shattered corpse of Kemp. This as Larry England, the silver star back on his vest, led the suddenly less voluble throng of townspeople out of the meeting hall. Where the shock of seeing that violent death had come again to Pomona caused the advance to slow.

'I'm fine, ma'am,' Edge assured her evenly. 'Surviving has gotten to be a habit with me. And when I quit, I don't plan for it to be this way.'

'Sir?' she queried, disinterested.

He spat out the offending piece of meat. And explained sardonically: 'Cold turkey.'

EDGE: THE LONER

by George G. Gilman

First in the Western series whose hero is the lone and sinister Edge – a new kind of Western hero, a man alone.

The idealised Westerner lives clean, is respectful to ladies, courteous to his social inferiors and gives his enemies a sporting chance.

Edge is not an idealised Westerner – not in any way at all. Look out for Edge.

NEW ENGLISH LIBRARY

EDGE: REVENGE RIDE

by George G. Gilman

Not even New Mexico buzzards can lick their lips. But these three were looking down, hungry-eyed, at their next meal.

Who stared right back at them, wide-eyed with horror.

Once, only a few hours ago, he'd fancied himself as a ladies' man. Until his last fancy turned out to be pretty much a ladies' lady.

He moved his head. Just his head. On account the outraged woman had buried him up to his neck and left him to die.

That was when the man called Edge knew he'd have to do some digging to get to the bottom of this story.

NEW ENGLISH LIBRARY

EDGE 50: SHADOW OF THE GALLOWS

by George G. Gilman

South of the border, down Sonora way, the old mission bells were silent, the old Spanish church, derelict, and the aged priest, travel-weary.

But he shared his wine with the man called Edge. Who, throat dry as an *arroyo* in high summer, was in great need. Needed also some time to recover from a night of Mexican mayhem. A campfire-lit horror show of gunned-down bandits, a mutilated *gringo* bounty hunter and his squaw, naked and dead on the bloodied ground.

NEW ENGLISH LIBRARY

EDGE MEETS STEELE: DOUBLE ACTION

by George G. Gilman

Not a whole lotta talkin' goin' on.

On account the two up top – driver and guard of the Central Western Stageline's Concord coach – were the strong silent type.

On account the younger woman inside was in deep mourning for her late lamented husband, the young man was of the Eastern and inscrutable persuasion, and the older woman believed in keeping herself to herself. Even if that was kinda difficult with the bucking, bolting Stage throwing them all together.

And the six Ute braves, war painted and feathered, who ambushed them didn't have polite conversation in mind either. Just killing.

Two others who'd never been great on idle chatter: Edge and Adam Steele. Who just happened to be riding within hearing distance of the gunshots and the screaming and knew that the time had come for some actions that spoke louder than words.

NEW ENGLISH LIBRARY

**Give them
the pleasure of choosing**

Book Tokens can be bought
and exchanged at most
bookshops in Great Britain
and Ireland.

THE EDGE SERIES BY GEORGE G. GILMAN FROM NEL